Duffle Bag Cartel 5

Lock Down Publications and Ca$h
Presents

Duffle Bag Cartel 5

A Novel by *Ghost*

Lock Down Publications
P.O. Box 944
Stockbridge, Ga 30281

Visit our website @
www.lockdownpublications.com

First Edition December 2020
Printed in the United States of America

This is a work of fiction. Names, characters, places, and incidents either are products of the author's imagination or are used fictitiously. Any similarity to actual events or locales or persons, living or dead, is entirely coincidental.

Lock Down Publications
Like our page on Facebook: Lock Down Publications
@
www.facebook.com/lockdownpublications.ldp
Cover design and layout by: **Dynasty Cover Me**
Book interior design by: **Shawn Walker**
Edited by: **Jill Alicea**

Stay Connected with Us!

Text **LOCKDOWN** to 22828 to stay up-to-date with new releases, sneak peaks, contests and more…
Thank you.

Submission Guideline.

Submit the first three chapters of your completed manuscript to ldpsubmissions@gmail.com, subject line: Your book's title. The manuscript must be in a .doc file and sent as an attachment. Document should be in Times New Roman, double spaced and in size 12 font. Also, provide your synopsis and full contact information. If sending multiple submissions, they must each be in a separate email.

Have a story but no way to send it electronically? You can still submit to LDP/Ca$h Presents. Send in the first three chapters, written or typed, of your completed manuscript to:

LDP: Submissions Dept
P.O. Box 944
Stockbridge, Ga 30281

DO NOT send original manuscript. Must be a duplicate.

Provide your synopsis and a cover letter containing your full contact information.

Thanks for considering LDP and Ca$h Presents.

Dedications:

First of all, this book is dedicated to my Baby Girl 3/10, the love of my life and purpose for everything I do. As long as I'm alive, you'll never want nor NEED for anything. We done went from flipping birds to flipping books. The best is yet to come.

To LDP'S CEO- Ca$h & COO- Shawn:

I would like to thank y'all for this opportunity. The wisdom, motivation, and encouragement that I've received from you two is greatly appreciated.

The grind is real. The loyalty in this family is real. I'm riding with LDP 'til the wheels fall off.

THE GAME IS OURS!

I GOT THE STREETS!

Chapter 1

Mikey stepped out into the hospital parking lot early Monday morning with a blue doctor's mask over his face and a brown paper bag full of medicine in his right hand. He still felt a bit sick, but the doctors had assured him that he was okay. His lungs felt like he was constantly inhaling little sharp pins, but the doctors had told him that the Coronavirus had attacked his lungs. They said that the feeling should go away within a few weeks, and he was hopeful.

He coughed and tried to swallow his spit. His throat was so dry. "Mane, where the fuck is this girl at?" he asked out loud, looking both ways. He needed to sit down. His head began to pound.

As if on cue, Ivy rounded the corner of the parking lot in her 2020 black on black Range Rover. She pulled in front of Mikey and popped the locks to the door. She was hoping that he wasn't in a foul mood. His last words to her before he had been quarantined was that he was going to kill her. She hoped that wasn't still on his mind.

Mikey opened the door and got into the truck. He pulled his seatbelt across his body and clicked it into place. "What's up with you?"

"I'm good. How are you feeling?" Ivy was trying to feel him out. He looked angry, as he always did. His long dreadlocks were nappy and all out of place.

"I'm feeling like I should kick yo' ass for having me admitted, and I would if they hadn't told me that you saved my life. Next time, when I tell yo' ratchet ass to do somethin', you listen to me, no matter the stakes. Do you understand that?"

"Yeah, I do, and you're welcome. I mean, if I wouldn't have done what I did, you wouldn't have been around to curse me out. Have you stopped to think about that?" She pulled out of the parking lot.

"That doesn't mean shit, Ivy. You're my bitch, and when I tell yo' ass to do something, you do it. You don't pick and choose what orders to follow and which ones not to follow. Shit don't work like that."

Ivy kept rolling. "Okay, next time I will just do what you say and not even think about how much I care about you." She shook her head in anger. "Anyway, you couldn't have gotten out of there at a better time. Memphis is going to shit, and the li'l so-called hustlers that you left out here to make those major moves for you ain't on nothin'. They were getting popped up and robbed left and right. It's ridiculous."

Mikey sat up in his seat. "What are you talking about? I ain't been down more than a month. How the fuck could shit fall off that much?"

She shrugged her shoulders. "I promise you, I don't know, but it's all bad. I'm just glad that you are home, and now we can get things back on track."

"You're right about that." Mikey pulled down the sun visor to block the harsh glare of the sun that was shining into his eyes, giving him a headache. He looked over the streets of Memphis while she drove. It felt like he was just getting out of prison, and in a sense, he kind of was. "What about my money? You were on top of my ends?"

"The few dope boys that are still loyal to you have been paying up. I stacked about a hundred G's for you since you were gone."

"A hundred G's? Bitch, are you kidding me? That ain't no ma'fuckin' money. You're saying we've been only pulling in twenty five G's a week? Really?"

"Please don't take this shit out on me. I told you that there are just a few dope boys that have been hitting you when they were supposed to. The few others that probably were looking to remain loyal to you were either shot up by those Duffle Bag Cartel thugs, or they were shot up by the Bread Gang and robbed. Smoke and his crew are out here running wild. This shit is madness. Oh, but then again, they just found the bodies of Tyson's wife and daughter, so I am thinking that somebody is even targeting the Bread Gang."

"The Bread Gang? Who the fuck is that? These niggas came out in just the few weeks I been down?"

"It's been more than a month, and yes. Smoke is their leader and them fools, Greedy and Tyson, were right behind him. I don't know what's up now, though, because ain't nobody heard from Smoke, Tyson, or Greedy. They ain't been on Facebook or none of that. I think Phoenix might be roaming through this bitch like the grim reaper."

"You mean to tell me that he ain't dead?" Mikey snapped.

"Not as far as I know, he ain't." Ivy pulled onto the expressway.

Suddenly the migraine that was flirting with Mikey came on full-fledged. There was a pounding sensation right behind his eyes. He rubbed his temples. "It's all good. I'ma figure this shit out. I always do. I should've known that Smoke was a snake, and I should've killed Phoenix when I had the chance, on multiple occasions. All of this derives from my fuck-ups, but it's good, though." He continued to rub his temples. "What about the good news? Do you have any of that?"

Ivy shook her head. "As sad as it is to say it, I really don't. Shit has been haywire since you were gone, and I only hope that you can get it all back on track without becoming a victim out here in these streets. I still love yo' black ass."

Mikey was in no mood to be lovey dovey. He was heated. If Ivy had only stacked a hundred thousand dollars while he was away, then that meant that he only had a little more than a million dollars to his name. In his mind, he was broke. There was no way that a true boss could run a major organization with only a million dollars to his name. He was so angry that he wanted to punch somebody. "So which one of my trap hoods been the most loyal?"

"Black Haven, baby. The Projects. The ma'fuckas over there, despite their adversity, have been making shit happen. Everybody still holds you up like you're the king of Black Haven. You gotta be grateful for that."

"And what about the Mound?" Orange Mound was his first homeland. He was born and bred there. "Who are they honoring harder than anybody else?"

"Well, you already know that Memphis belongs to the legacy of Taurus as a whole. The Orange Mound is no different. If you roll through there, you'll see all kinds of pictures of Taurus painted on the walls, because his birthday was just on April the twenty-seventh. But after him, they are hollering Smoke. They say that Smoke is the king of Orange Mound, and he's taking that shit to the head. At least, I think he is. Ain't nobody see him in a few days."

Mikey grunted. "Yeah, we're about to see about all of that. Roll me to a few of the traps and let me collect some of my bread so I can show these niggas that I am alive and well. After I connect a few loose ends, I see I got some heads to bust, so that'll be priority number two. But for now, let's roll, baby. We got a lot of work to do."

"Cool, Mikey, you already know I'm riding wit' you until the bitter end." Ivy stepped on the gas.

***

Natalia opened the front door to her mansion and took a step back. "Please come in, and thank you for coming."

Alicia slowly walked inside with her Birkin bag in her hand. She side-eyed Natalia and kept walking. "I'm still trying to figure out why you couldn't tell me what was good over the phone. Why do you need for me to come and holler at you in person?"

Natalia closed the door to the mansion and locked it. "As a woman, I feel like there is a bit of animosity between you and I, and I just want to get a nice understanding with you. That way, we can go on with our lives. So if you don't mind, I have prepared a nice steak dinner with all of the fixings and got out a bottle of aged wine from the early nineteen hundreds collection. Phoenix is out of town, and Sabrina has both the baby and Shante. We are free to be grownups and to speak freely. So you can say whatever you feel, and it's all good."

"Awright. I think that you are a petty bitch for naming your son after mine. You knew that my son was supposed to be Phoenix's junior, and because those whack jobs took him away from me, you hijacked his name. You are a petty bitch, and that's how I feel."

"Okay, I see that we are kicking this off quite early. Well, Alicia, if that's how you really feel, I think that you are a straight slut, and Phoenix would never have been in this position if you would've known how to keep your legs closed. You are a whore, and I don't give a fuck what you wanted to name your child. I'ma name mine after his father, and my future husband."

"Bitch, that is your cousin, and if you ever do try to marry him, they are going to lock yo' stupid ass up. That ain't happening. And since you think I'm a slut, I'ma just tell you what I think of you."

"Will you, now?" Natalia crossed her arms. "Well, let me hear this."

"Bitch, you are an incest queen. Your self-esteem is so low that you gotta fuck wit' a nigga in yo' family, just because you already know another nigga would dog yo' yellow ass. You're mixed, and you still ain't all that. I can guarantee you bought that ass and those thick lips you got on your face. That shit ain't real. But I guess when you get a hold of the right amount of cash, you can be whatever you wanna be."

Now Natalia was offended. "Everything on me is real. It either comes from my mother…" She pulled on her long hair and pointed to her crystal blue eyes. "Or it comes from my father's side of the family." She hoisted up her breasts and smacked her fat ass. It jiggled. "And with all of that weave in your head, you should be the last one to talk about what's real and what's fake, because all of your shit is fake."

Alicia stepped into her face. "You think that you're all of that, don't you?"

Natalia smiled. "You have no idea all of what I really am. If you knew who you were standing in front of, you would bow down and honor me. I am that bitch. Trust and believe, I was that way before Lizzo."

"Bitch, change yo' son's name. I'm not playing wit' you."

"Fuck you. Kiss my mixed ass."

Alicia slapped her as hard as she could and tackled her to the ground. "Change that baby's name. Phoenix Jr. was my son." She got ready to punch Natalia in the face.

Natalia rolled her off of her and hopped up. She dabbed her finger to the corner of her mouth and looked at the blood there. She spit it on the carpet. "That was the last time that you ever put your hands on me." She pulled a serrated knife from the small of her back.

Alicia took a step back and looked for a weapon. "Bitch, why you gotta pull out a blade and shit? What, you're scared to throw these thangs?" She pulled the lamp from the table and held it up before yanking the cord out of the wall.

Natalia placed her ass-length hair into a knot and rolled her head around on her shoulder. "One of us is not about to leave this room alive. Unlike you, I got a child to live for, so I plan on making it out on the other side." She rushed Alicia at full speed and jumped in the air. She slammed the knife into the upper portion of her shoulder and twisted it.

"Arrrrghhh." Alicia screamed at the top of her lungs.

Natalia took the knife out and swept Alicia's feet from under her with a floor round house. Alicia fell, and she rolled on top of her. She smacked her with her right hand and slammed the knife into her shoulder again. Alicia wailed, leaned up, and head butted Natalia off of her. Natalia could feel the blood pouring out of her nose. She laughed and stood up. Alicia pulled the knife out of her shoulder and held it as a weapon.

Natalia laughed. "You sure you're ready to fight until the death? Huh, bitch? You better remember that I have two legacies that war constantly inside of my blood. There is the crazy Russian blood that seeks to conquer the world. It is cold. It is calculating. It is relentless, and smart. Then there is my father Taurus's blood. It is unforgiving. It is savage. It is merciless." She stepped into the kitchen and grabbed a machete from the pantry that she'd hidden there. The metal blade shined in the kitchen light. She stepped back into the living room. "Are you ready, Alicia?"

Alicia looked her over with hatred. "You muthafuckin' right, I am."

Alicia took off running toward Natalia with the knife in her hand. She raised it over her head. She fixed her eyes on Natalia's chest. She saw herself plunging the knife deep into Natalia. But before she could plant it, Natalia side-stepped her and swung the machete with all of her might. It slammed into the base of Alicia's throat and cut into the meat there.

Alicia felt like she'd been hit in the throat by an axe. She choked and dropped her knife. Her hands went to her bleeding neck. She struggled to get up.

Natalia circled her. "This is for Mother Russia." She swung the machete and sliced a huge chunk out of Alicia's neck, knocking Alicia to the ground. She walked closer. "Get up, bitch! Talk that bullshit now."

Whack.

The blade opened Alicia so much that blood was spurting everywhere like a geyser. Natalia became excited by the blood. She raised the machete and brought it down again and then again. She became giddy, whacking Alicia over and over. "Die, bitch. Die."

Alicia jumped up and tried her best to run to the front door. Natalia ran behind her and sliced the back of her neck, skeeting blood across the couch and the paintings on the wall. Alicia fell to her knees. She placed her hand over the large wound. Blood seeped through her fingers and dripped off of her wrist and elbow. "Why? Why are you doing this to me?" She stumbled and stood up with her shirt drenched in her own blood. Her eyes crossed. She was lightheaded.

Natalia walked up on her with the machete dripping. "Any woman that Phoenix loves will meet this fate. There is no room in his heart for anybody other than me. I am for him only."

A line of blood squirted from Alicia's neck. She grew weak in the knees. "You can have him. I don't want him. Please just let me get to a hospital. I will never fuck with y'all again." She fell to her knees, woozy.

"In Russia, we finish what we started. You are prey. Die, bitch, and say hi to your son for me. Here is a secret: I paid to have your ugly son killed, and it was the delight of my life." She laughed for a moment, then her eyes turned low and menacing. She raised the machete to finish Alicia.

"You bitch."

With one last burst of energy Alicia hopped from the floor and tackled Natalia into the china cabinet, shattering it. Games popped into the air and settled around both of their bodies. Alicia landed on top of Natalia and punched her three times with her bloody fist. She became too weak to finish her.

Natalia screamed and swung the machete with all of her might. It lodged itself into Alicia's neck so far that blood ran out of her throat like a broken faucet. She died before her head hit the hardwood floor. Natalia slid from under her and stomped her face.

"Only I will mother Phoenix's son." Her chest heaved up and down.

She called her clean up men to dispose of Alicia's body, and then jumped in the shower with a sadistic smile on her face.

Ghost

Chapter 2

Smoke walked through the State fairgrounds with his arm around Precious. He kissed her cheek and kept strolling. It was a hot and humid day, and the Tennessee State Fair was crowded and jumping. Smoke had already won Precious two huge stuffed animals and was thinking about winning her a third, even though she was having a hard time carrying the ones that she had. She was growing on him as a woman. He felt himself becoming enamored by her, and for some unforeseen reason, he didn't want her out of his presence.

He kissed her cheek again as he navigated her through the crowd of people. "Baby, are you enjoying yourself?"

Precious nodded. "Yeah, this joint lit. I feel like I ain't never had this much fun. Thank you for bringing me out and for spending so much time wit' me, Smoke. I know you are a very busy man and you could've been anywhere else, but you're here with me. I appreciate that." She kissed his cheek.

"Long as you know who daddy is." He smiled and held her tighter within his embrace.

"I do, and he lived back in Houston." She snickered.

"Aw, that's how you gon' do me?"

"That's just how I'm gon' do you. We might be kicking it a li'l bit, but you ain't reached that daddy status just yet. I keep waiting for you to turn on me and go back to the ways that everybody and they mama that know you say you gon' go back to. I mean, it's been lovely so far, but you're sure that once I give you this li'l kitty, you aren't going to turn on me?"

Smoke flared his nostrils. "Shawty, what I tell you about listening to other niggas? Didn't I tell you that shit like that will ruin us fast? Now you need to rock wit' me the long way and judge me off of how I carry myself every single day. Fuck everybody else. Everybody else ain't flying to Dubai wit' me at the end of the week, are they?"

She shook her head. "Not that I know of."

"A'ight den. Fuck wit' me." He gripped her ass and pulled her closer to him.

Precious hugged his waist. "So what else is on our agenda for today? Are we just going to keep playing games until I get too many stuffed animals to carry, or are we going to go back to your place, and you can finally buss me down? I think I might be feenin' for you." She batted her eyelashes. "And, I mean, you have earned it."

Smoke gripped her ass a little harder, imagining what it would be like to finally fuck Precious. He'd been so close over the last few weeks, but had decided to back off to see if he could have enough discipline to treat her differently than how he had treated every other female before. It was driving him insane because Precious was so bad to him, especially physically. And even though she was only eighteen years old, she carried herself like a true boss. He liked that.

"Look at you being all excited." She laughed. "So do you wanna get out of here right now, or what?"

"Let's grab a slice first, and then we'll bounce." He guided her to the pizza stand and stood in a lengthy line.

Precious stood in front of him and backed up so that her ass was on his front. "Have you decided what you're going to make me yet? I was thinking of a bottle girl. I know they are saying that you have to be twenty-one to handle the liquor, but ain't nobody gonna be all up in our business like that. If I was a bottle girl, I would be able to promote the club with class and elegance. I also know how to be flirtatious and how to give the club just that overall feeling of sexy. The stripper thing is cool, but after you get a hold of this gap, you ain't gon want me grinding all up on other men. Besides, what would make me so special to you after that if I did do that? Niggas would be looking at you like you're stupid."

"Fuck would they be doing that for?" He moved them forward in the line.

"Because they would know how all of this ass feel, and they would be able to pay to see what your woman feels like back there. Niggas be doing that shit just to live in your shoes for a minute. You know how that shit go." She looked up at him. "I'm my daddy's girl. I don't want nobody touching on me but you. That's just how I feel."

Smoke tensed his muscles and became seriously possessive of her. "Well, you damn sure ain't about to be stripping for nobody other than me. So you can get that shit out of your mind." He stepped up to the window, ordered them two slices of pizza, paid for it, and was handed the food. He gave her one and took the other. They walked away from the window.

"My girl just sent me a screenshot of that Black Haven nigga Mikey's Rolls Royce Phantom. I guess he's back in Memphis, and everywhere he is rolling, he got like three vans following him. This screenshot was in North Memphis. I heard you used to fuck wit' him, but y'all are beefing now. What's good wit' that?"

"Shit happens. Fuck that nigga. If he rolls around through the city now, then it's time for his sucka ass to get smoked. Pun intended." Smoke felt himself becoming heated. "Come on, let's roll out to my pad so I can see what my baby is working wit'." He dropped his pizza to the ground and took the teddy bears out of her hands.

***

Phoenix stepped into the basement and placed a pair of black latex gloves on his hands. He took a pair of pliers out of the tool box and stepped up to a sleeping Tyson. Tyson's face was swollen from the constant ass whooping that he'd received from Phoenix and his cold-hearted henchmen. Phoenix slapped Tyson across the face and jarred him awake.

"Wake yo' punk ass up."

Tyson awoke hollering into the duct tape. His eyes were blackened. Sweat and blood ran down his face. He began to shake like crazy.

"Li'l nigga, Ayesha is dead. Eliza is dead. And some li'l white girl with blonde hair is dead. Greedy was fuckin' the shit out of your daughter - if that's your daughter. And, well, the shit hit the fan. It is what it is. Have you spoken to Greedy since he was chained next to you?"

Tyson shook his head. He hollered into the tape in emotional agony. He didn't know if what Phoenix was saying was the truth, but if it was, it was devastating news. He couldn't imagine himself not being able to be with Ayesha anymore, or Eliza. They were both his world, despite the looming paternity of Eliza.

Phoenix snatched the duct tape off of his mouth. "Fuck you trying to say?"

"Come on, Phoenix, man. Please tell me that you didn't kill my family. Please, man. Tell me what type of dirty game you're playing? Those were my babies." He cried.

"Hands down, you the ugliest crying nigga I ever seen. Yo' face all wrinkled and shit. Dawg, cut that shit out, because I feel nothing. Straight up. Yo' people dead. Yo' bitch and my goddaughter. Oh well. He was fucking Eliza. That li'l bitch was naked as hell when I got there. Mmm. Her body was righteous, too. What a waste."

Tyson looked over to Greedy. "You was fucking my daughter, bitch-ass nigga?"

Phoenix ripped the tape off of Greedy's mouth as well. "Respond, nigga."

"Don't act like you ain't thought about fuckin' that li'l bitch, too. She walked around with her li'l fresh ass poked all the way out, with them fat-ass titties. Nipples all big and shit. Hell yeah, I fucked on multiple occasions." He closed his eyes. "Best pussy I ever had too. I got no regrets, other than this shit. Caught a nigga slipping wit' his pants down. Fuck."

"She was fifteen, nigga. Fifteen! What the fuck is wrong with you?" Tyson snapped.

"Well, I grew her li'l ass up quick. She came to me a virgin and inexperienced as a muthafucka. It was so cute. But by the time she left me, she was riding me and taking the dick. Eating pussy and every thang. Damn, that was my li'l bitch." Greedy started to get hard from just thinking about it.

Tyson went crazy within his bonds. He yanked at the chains that held his wrists in place. "I'ma kill you, Greedy. You bitch-ass nigga! You ain't nothing but a predator. That's it. A low life, hype-ass predator."

Greedy shrugged his shoulders. "I like coochie, nigga. Every man in the world likes coochie. I just stick to young hoes. I can't help it. Bury me a predator den." He closed his eyes.

"Tyson, since I really don't think you had much to do with my son's death, I'm going to do you a favor." Phoenix knelt down and picked up two small axes with long handles. He took them and set them on the table.

"Oh yeah? What are you going to do for me, Phoenix?" Tyson mugged him, and then the axes.

"I'm finna let you get your revenge on Greedy. I'ma give you an axe, and I'ma let you beat his ass to death with it." Phoenix snickered.

"What? That shit ain't fair. I ain't kill yo' baby, either. That shit ain't have nothing to do with me." Greedy was nervous.

"Y'all already know I don't like neither one of you bitch-ass niggas. So Greedy, I'ma give you one too. You get to fuck him up as well. The last man standing will get a surprise." Phoenix motioned for his huge bodyguards to come and release one of each of Tyson and Greedy's hands. Once they were released, an axe was placed into each hand, but the bodyguard held the hand until Phoenix backed away. "Now you niggas are side by side. It's even. One of you will die. Good luck. Release they bitch asses."

As soon as the guards moved, Greedy swung his axe and planted it directly into Tyson's chest. It got stuck and crushed his breastplate. Tyson hollered like a wounded wolf. He swung his axe and slammed it into Greedy's ear. The blade cut through the side of his face. He refused to holler, even though he was in excruciating pain. He yanked his axe out of Tyson's chest, and swung it again. This time it connected with Tyson's forehead and killed him immediately. He pulled it out and swung it again and again. Then he dropped the axe, breathing hard.

Phoenix nodded. "Now that's how you kill a ma'fucka." Phoenix took his head and slammed it with all of his might into the brick wall behind him over and over again with a scowl on his face. He slammed it until the back of Greedy's head flattened and the life left out of him. Then he stepped back.

"Two down, two to go."

***

Natalia tossed and turned inside of the king-sized bed. She kept having one nightmare after the next, and she felt hotter than usual. She kicked the blankets off of her body and sat up in bed. There was a constant knocking on her front door. She got out of the bed and wrapped her robe around her body. She took her .9 millimeter from under her pillow and made haste to the front door. She checked the security cameras and saw the back of a large figure standing at her door. She cocked her gun and pulled the door open. She was about to raise the pistol and place it into the man's face when suddenly his eyes became familiar. He pulled his hood back.

"Daddy? Is that you?" She felt her stomach flip over twice.

Taurus held a finger to his lips and nodded. "Baby girl, they know that I am alive now. You are in danger. We need to talk." He stepped inside along with four masked Jamaican assassins and took ahold of her into his arms.

Natalia hugged him and began to cry. "Okay, Daddy. Let's talk. Thank you, God. Let's talk."

Chapter 3

Precious stepped into the bedroom and pulled open her red satin Victoria's Secret sheer robe. She looked across the room at Smoke as he dropped his Ferragamo pants and stepped out of them. He took his pistol and hid it under the pillow that he was going to lay his head on, then stood and eyed Precious from across the room.

Precious closed the bedroom door and licked her succulent lips. "You think you're ready for me, daddy?"

Smoke stepped out of his boxers and grabbed ahold of his piece. "Since the first day I met you. Now bring yo' li'l fine ass here and let me see what that thang is about." He walked over to her.

Precious met him in the center of the room beside the bed. She wrapped her arms around his neck and kissed all over his lips. "You better take it easy on me. Mmm. You know this is my first time." She kissed him some more.

Smoke squeezed her ass and rubbed all over it. It felt soft and hefty to the touch. He bit her neck. "I'm from the Orange Mound, shawty. We don't ever take it easy on nobody." He bit into her neck and picked her up. He threw her on the bed and climbed between her thighs. His hand went right between her legs. He felt her hot, squishy sex lips. The cloth was already damp. This made him shiver. "Damn, boo."

Precious licked all over his lips. "Taste me, daddy. Please, I need you to taste me."

Smoke climbed out of the bed and stood back. His four gold ropes swung around on his neck. "We finna do this shit like we supposed to. I'm finna make yo' first time the best time and get on that boss shit wit' you." He left out of her sight and went into the closet. After moving back to the wall, he pulled out two Duffle bags of cash that he had yet to count.

He took one stuffed bag and dumped the money on top of Precious. Then he picked up the other and did the same thing. Five hundred thousand dollars in cash fell all over her and the bed. He climbed back on top of her and forced her knees backward, exposing her pussy through the panties. He kissed the juicy lips. "Now we finna get on that shit, shawty." He pulled the material to the side and began to eat her like a savage.

Precious yelped and began to moan loudly. "Uhhhh, shit! Shit, Smoke! Uhhhh, daddy." She felt Smoke licking in between her folds hungrily. He trapped her clit and twirled his tongue around it, sending tremors throughout her body. She began to gasp over and over. His tongue went deeply into her, and she humped into it.

Smoke inhaled her scent, and it drove him wild. He flicked his tongue faster and faster. He felt her tense up. "Uh-huh. Uh-huh. Cum, bitch. Cum." He nibbled on her clit and sucked on it.

Precious hollered and came hard. "Aw shit, daddy! Aw shit! Oooh!" She fell back on the bed.

Smoke kissed her pussy one last time, and then he got between her thighs. He rubbed her slit. "I'm finna buss this shit down. You already know that you're my baby. It's been a long time coming." He grabbed his piece and began to work the head into her sex lips.

Precious moaned and grabbed the gun from under the pillow. She cocked it nonchalantly, brought it out, and aimed it at Smoke. "Get yo' bitch ass off of me."

Boom!

The bullet smacked into Smoke's chest and knocked him backward. He fell to the floor, completely taken off guard. His eyes were bucked. He placed his hand over the gunshot wound to make sure that it was indeed there. "Fuck." He was dazed. He used the bed to stand up.

Precious threw her dress over her head and mugged Smoke. "Daddy, I told you this nigga was a goofy."

Mikey slid into the room laughing. "Turn coat-ass nigga. One way you can always get a ma'fucka to slip is by use of a bitch's pussy. This shit is hilarious. Look at all of this money. My ma'fuckin' money! Simple-ass nigga."

Precious came over to Mikey and kissed his lips. "What do you want me to do?"

Mikey moved her to the side. "Nigga, step yo' ass out of this room. You're bleeding all over my money. I don't like that."

Smoke was struggling to breathe. The bullet that entered into him had pierced his left lung. "Fuck you, Mikey." He took a deep breath.

Mikey shook his head. "Nawl, it ain't no fuck me, Smoke, you can't do that. Just like you can't fuck my bitch. You's a goofy."

Precious came forward and aimed her gun. "Let me smoke this fool, daddy. Let me show him that we get down in Houston, just like they get down out here in Memphis. But the women run Houston. It's time niggas realize that shit, too."

Houston was set to be Mikey's new stomping grounds. He'd made a lot of connections out that way, one of the major connections being Rivera himself. Rivera had given him the lowdown on Smoke, and Mikey used it to his benefit. Mikey stepped up to Smoke. "Where is Phoenix?"

Smoke was woozy. "Fuck you, and fuck Phoenix. Fuck both of you niggas." He horked and spit directly into Mikey's face.

Precious sidestepped Mikey and finger fucked her trigger. "Nasty-ass nigga."

Boom! Boom! Boom! Boom!

Smoke took the bullets and ran past them with Precious on his ass. Boom! A bullet hit his back. Boom! Another his right arm. Boom! Another popped the back of his neck and turned him around. Precious jumped up and kicked him in the chest. He flew backward.

She pressed the barrel to his forehead. "Gang. Gang." Boom! Boom! Boom!

His brains blew out the back of his head. A puddle of blood formed around him. He jerked on the carpet. His bodyguards stood around him as the life dissipated from his body. They looked up at Mikey, who they honored as the rightful leader of the Duffle Bag Cartel.

Mikey looked down on Smoke's body. "You muthafuckas pay attention, because this is what disloyalty looks like. Clear this bitch out. Every ounce of my money in here, get it, and let's go. We're out of here in five minutes." He pulled Precious to him and tongued her down.

***

"Natalia." Shante ran into the mansion and wrapped her arms around Natalia's waist. She hugged her tightly. "I missed you so much." The light from the sun coming through the window reflected off of Shante's forehead. She smiled up at Natalia. "Where is my brother? Can I see him?"

Natalia nodded her head. "You sure can, baby. He's upstairs in the nursery. Go on up. There is somebody up there that wants to meet you anyway." She spoke in terms of her father, Taurus.

"Okay." She hugged Natalia again and headed upstairs to the nursery.

Natalia smiled until Shante got to the top of the stairs, and then her face turned to a scowl. She stepped onto the brick porch and eyed Sabrina sitting in her Lexus truck, scrolling down the call log of her phone. Instead of calling out to her, she stepped back into the mansion and grabbed her Chanel bag. She went back outside and opened Sabrina's truck door. She placed the Chanel bag on the floor under the seat.

"Hey girl, what you doing?"

"I'm just finishing this last text." Sabrina was answering the last questions from Kevin in regards to the federal investigation that was being launched by his department. So far, she had made sure that she hadn't left anything out. Kevin had made it perfectly clear that it was in her best interest to tell the department everything that they needed to know in regards to Phoenix's crimes and the operations of the Duffle Bag Cartel. She did what she could, and she prayed that it was enough to keep her from being indicted for whatever reason.

"Oh. Anyway, I just wanted to come down and say hi. Thank you for keeping an eye on Shante. I know she has been keeping you busy. I should be able to keep my eye on her from here on out. I don't want her around no snitch anyway." Natalia glared at her.

Sabrina was in mid-text. She froze when she heard those words. She looked over to Natalia. "Snitch? What are you talking about?"

"Nothin'. I'm just playin' wit' you girl. Well, I betta get back in here. I'll see bits of you later." She climbed out of the truck and closed the door.

"You'll see bits of me later? What does that mean?" Sabrina hollered out of the window.

"It's a Russian term. Don't worry about it." Natalia jogged into the mansion and eyed Sabrina before she closed the door.

Sabrina started the ignition and pulled out of the driveway. She waited until she was out of the gated community before she called Kevin's direct number. He picked up on the fourth ring.

"Kevin, I think Natalia may be on to me. She called me a snitch!" she hollered into the phone.

"Impossible. There is no way that she could possibly know that you are working with us. The investigation has been held tightly to all of our chests," he assured her.

"Well, something doesn't seem right. Her exact words were that she didn't want Shante hanging around with a snitch."

Kevin was quiet for a moment. "Those were the words she used?"

"Exactly. What do you think that means?" Sabrina entered on the freeway and picked up speed.

"It sounds like it means you're screwed."

"What?" Sabrina felt her heart skip a beat.

"The life of a snitch is always temporary!" he hollered in Russian.

Sabrina looked down at her phone. "But you said—"

Boom!

The Lexus truck blew into a ball of fire and shot into the air, where it separated into a bunch of little pieces. They sailed to the ground on fire. The cars on the expressway swerved around them. Some crashed, trying to avoid the blaze, while others escaped with no injury.

***

Natalia took her thumb off of the detonation device and laughed. She could see the black cloud in the sky ten miles out. She knew it was Sabrina. She wired the hundred thousand dollars into Kevin's offshore account and closed the door to her mansion. "All that Phoenix loved before me will perish," she whispered.

***

Mikey grabbed the last duffle bag and tossed it to his head of security. The goon took the bag and stuffed it, along with the others, into the black van that was headed to Houston, Texas, where Mikey was going to reassemble and reestablish the new Duffle Bag Cartel. The van had a total of six million dollars in cash. For Mikey, that was a good start for a new location.

He'd already staked his claim to a few of the project buildings in Clover Land. They were in need of quality narcotics, and his plug with Rivera was going to make sure that he kept both Memphis and Houston on lock. All of Smoke's crew had switched over to him, and Black Haven's goons pledged their allegiance to him as well. All in all, Mikey was certain that it was impossible for him to lose, especially since the Duffle Bag Cartel had two judges and a senator on the payroll.

Ivy came beside him and kissed his neck. "I'm so happy. We can finally leave Memphis alone for a little while. Things are going to be so much better in Houston." She kissed his neck again and loaded into his Range Rover.

Mikey cheesed as he watched his workers getting everything in position to travel. When they were done, they stood in place, looking for his next command. Mikey liked that power. He held his hand up.

"Everybody, let's go. Houston is the next stop."

***

Mikey and the Duffle Bag Cartel members that he was relocating to the Houston chapter arrived in Houston five hours later. Mikey pulled the Range Rover into a rundown Clover Land Project building and nodded his head when he saw fifty members of the Duffle Bag Cartel already waiting in the parking lot for him. He could feel the excitement of the power flowing through his veins. He snickered. "This that shit I'm talking about right here. You see dis shit, baby?" He continued to look over the animals that were crowding around his truck.

Ivy reached under the seat and grabbed the Mach Uzi. She slammed it to the side of his head. "You's a dumb-ass nigga."

Mikey held his hands up. "What the fuck is you doing?"

Phoenix stepped through the crowd of Duffle Bag Cartel killas and slid the shotgun to Mikey's temple. "Bitch nigga, you could never run my shit. I *am* the Duffle Bag Cartel king. Rest in blood, nigga."

Boom!

Chapter 4
Seven months later

It was a dark and stormy night in September. The thunder in Houston roared boisterously outside as Phoenix lowered the blood-colored Coronavirus mask under his chin and picked up the pliers from the table, opening and closing them with an evil sneer on his face. He looked over his shoulder at the light-skinned dope boy that was seconds away from potentially facing the worst punishment that he ever had in his young life.

Phoenix shook his head and laughed to himself. "Say, li'l nigga, I don't know how Mikey used to run shit back in Memphis, but dis ain't that, homeboy. You got 'bout ten seconds to tell me where the fuck my chips at or you gon' regret ever picking up a sack under this Cartel." He turned around so that he was now facing him inside of the small basement, which was filthy with spiderwebs in every nook and cranny of it.

The medium-sized dope boy struggled against his bonds. He hollered into the duct tape as sweat slid down the side of his face. His stomach felt in knots, and he begged for the chance to plead his case one more time. He tossed his head back and began to talk through the covering over his mouth as if Phoenix could really hear or understand what he was saying.

Phoenix stepped forward and ripped the tape from his face. With a backward motion, he slapped him so hard that he spit blood into the air. Phoenix grabbed him by the jaws. "You got somethin' you wanna say to me?"

"Phoenix, that's what Jimmy Bands dropped off to me. As soon as he pulled off, you pulled up, and I handed you yo' cheese. Whatever the count is ain't got shit to do wit' me man, damn! Why the fuck am I the only nigga down here?" Blood ran out of his nostrils and along his lips. It coupled with the snot that was already there.

Phoenix mugged him and knelt down just enough so that both men were eye level. “You tryna tell me something without actually telling me?”

He avoided eye contact with him. “Look, mane, I'm just saying that whatever foul shit going on ain't got shit to do wit’ me, and everythang to do with whoever you got stacking yo’ cheese for you when you ain't in Houston. I ain't nobody but a collector. My job is to have the bread for you when you get here, but I can only give you what they give me.” He struggled to breathe. His breaths came out in ragged squeaks.

Phoenix stood up and rubbed his chin for a second. “Only ma’fucka I got collecting my scratch and dropping it off to you so that you can have it when I get there is Jimmy Bands. I’ve known li'l homie since he was eight years old. You insinuating that my li'l nigga dipping in my shit?”

“Whoa, whoa, whoa, I ain't saying shit like that. I'm only saying that I don't have anything to do wit’ yo’ shorts, and I don't like how you tryna hold me responsible. That shit weak. You gotta get yo’ house in order, and that shit don't start wit’ me, but wit them other niggas. I'm low level.”

Phoenix nodded his head. He tried to think logically. His eyes pinned on a random spot on the wall and kept it while his thoughts ran rampant. He'd know Jimmy Bands for what seemed like an eternity. He had watched him grow up in Orange Mound and had even hit his mother Sheila on numerous occasions with money just to make sure that Jimmy and his younger sister Skyy ate at night. If the dope boy was insinuating what he thought he was, then Phoenix felt he would be left with no choice other than to murder Jimmy Bands in a slow, torturous way.

“I'd have to be crazy to even think about fucking wit’ yo’ scratch, Phoenix. Every nigga and they mama already know how you get down in these streets. I'm only eighteen, mane.

Dat's too young to die, plus you got me checking a bag for just holding ya shit until you come and get it. Fuck I look like burning dat bridge?" The dope boy spit bloody mucus onto the concrete.

Phoenix lowered his head and stepped back directly in front of the young hustler. "Say, li'l potna, you betta be telling me the truth, 'cause if you ain't, I'm 'bout to really fuck some shit up. Don't forget, that fool Mikey had you starving. I got you making a few G's a week to basically do nothing, not to mention all the other li'l side money you be catching on the back end because of me. When a ma'fucka bite this hand, I can't do shit but respond accordingly. So we finna get to the bottom of dis right now." Phoenix pulled his phone from his pocket and began to text Jimmy Bands. He told him that they had a situation, and that his presence was needed immediately. "There, that's how we finna do that."

The dope boy lowered his head. "You already know that fool ain't about to admit to nothing. Everybody know you crazy, mane. Where da fuck that gon' leave me?"

"I'm missing twenty G's over the last three weeks. Somebody finna tell me something, or I'm smoking both of you niggas and filling yo positions. You know how many niggas out here that would give their right arms to be down with the Duffle Bag Cartel? Huh?"

"Yeah, I do. Shid, I'm one of those niggas. I wasn't on shit before you gave me a chance. That's why I'm telling you that I would never cross you on no level. My loyalty is everythang, mane. Dis shit can't fall on me."

As he finished his last sentence, Jimmy Bands made his way down the steps of the basement. He was heavyset and dark-skinned with deep waves and a handsome face. His entire grill was shiny gold, and his eyebrows were thick and almost connected. When he saw Phoenix he smiled and stepped off of the last stair. He looked to his right and saw the state of the dope boy and a slow mug came over his face.

Phoenix walked right up to him with anger written all over his face. “I'm missing twenty G’s in three weeks. This ma’fucka right here say it gotta be you ’cause you dropped off the money within minutes before I pulled up. Is this true?”

Five Duffle Bag Cartel hittas stepped out of the shadows and stood behind Phoenix with black leather gloves on their hands. Each savage awaited the word from Phoenix to crush either Jimmy Bands or the bound dope boy, or both.

Jimmy Bands upped his Glock Forty and pressed the barrel to the young dope boy's head. “Bitch nigga, dis what you doing after I brought you over to the mob? I figured as much.” He frowned and pulled the trigger twice.

The dope boy's brains burst out of the back of his head and splattered the walls. He slumped forward with blood running down his neck. His bowels released themselves, and the heavy scent of gunpowder and burnt flesh wafted into the air of the basement.

Phoenix stepped over to the slain man and looked down on him. “Fuck you do that for? Nigga, I ain't tell you to crush him. I make the decisions around here, and I ain't tell you to do shit.” Phoenix upped his .45 and cocked it, and because he did, his security crew behind him upped their weapons as well.

Jimmy Bands tucked his gun back into his holster. “Say, mane, I ain't accepting no fuck nigga putting dat thurr jacket on me. I'm from the Mound, shawty, and a ma’fucka name all he got. ’Sides all dat, dat fuck nigga was lying.”

Phoenix stepped into his face. “Oh yeah? Well, how the fuck I know dat, huh? How the fuck I know he wasn't telling the truth, and because he was, you thought it was smart to dead his ass?” Phoenix stuffed his gun under Jimmy Bands' chin, ready to blow his brains out next. “Answer me!”

Jimmy Bands mugged Phoenix and flared his nostrils. "Phoenix, you my big potna. Dis baring arms against each other ain't for us, mane. We already at war wit' dem Bread Gang niggas, and it's a few rogues out there that's coming at the Cartel that were real loyal to Mikey, so we need to be focused on dat, and not dis shit right hurr."

Phoenix grabbed Jimmy Bands by the throat and slammed him into the wall. He pulled back the hammer on his gun and pressed the barrel to Jimmy's forehead. "Money over everythang, nigga! You got five seconds to explain yo'self. Four now."

Jimmy winced in emotional hurt. He looked into Phoenix's eyes and whistled. "Bring her down."

Seconds later, the steps began to squeak with heavy footsteps. A dark-skinned masked female came down the steps with a small Dollar Tree bag in one hand and her left arm wrapped around an older white lady's neck. The lady's mouth was duct taped. She tossed the lady to the floor and threw the plastic bag containing thirty-one thousand dollars to Phoenix.

Phoenix caught the bag with one hand and kept his gun on Jimmy. He threw the bag to his closest security guard, Big Hurk, a three hundred pound, dark-skinned, ex-NFL offensive lineman.

"Potna, open dat shit, and tell me what it is." He turned back to Jimmy. "Who is that white bitch?"

"That's the dead nigga's mama. He been tearing yo' ass off little by little and giving the chips to his ole girl. We tore that bitch crib up for thirty minutes until she finally took us to the stash and admitted what her son been doing. Both their asses should be held responsible, if you ask me." He mugged the older woman. "Now can you please remove this gun from my forehead?"

"What's in dat bag?" Phoenix called over his shoulder at Big Hurk.

"Cash, homie, and a lot of it. Just by eyeballing dis shit I can say that it's every bit of twenty five or thirty G's." Big Hurk closed the bag back.

Phoenix lowered his gun, and an evil smile came over his face. "I never doubted you, shawty. But you already know dat business is business. Technically you introduced me to dis thief, so in every other mob, you would be just as responsible. Call yo'self getting off light." He snatched the bag from Hurk and began to eyeball the money.

Jimmy Bands lowered his eyes and rubbed his forehead. He felt ill will toward Phoenix. Nobody had ever so much as upped a gun on him without pulling the trigger and lived to tell about it. Visions of murdering Phoenix in cold blood caused his heart to beat at a rapid pace. Instead of exposing his hand of hatred, he fixed his clothes and upped his gun again. He stepped over the fallen dope boy's mother and placed his foot on her chest. She yelped and closed her eyes.

"Bitch, yo' son almost got my life taken. You gave birth to him, so you just as guilty. Rest in peace."

"Wait!" Phoenix yelled.

Boom! Boom!

Jimmy Bands took a step back and marveled at his handiwork. A broad smile came over his face. "Fuck that bitch! Next chapter."

Phoenix stood over her and assessed the situation. He tightened his grip on the bag of cash. "Damn, nigga, you can't just go around killing ma'fuckas without my go ahead. You run under me. Understand what dat mean?"

Jimmy looked over his kill and slowly trailed his eyes up to meet Phoenix's. "Yeah, boss, I understand what that mean, but they had to pay. Blood is the only payment." He tucked his gun. “You got yo’ money and the situation cleaned itself up. May I be excused?”

Phoenix stepped into his face. “You made the mess on dis trap floor, so you gon' clean it up. Once you finish wit’ that, you get back on yo’ grind because time is money, and we lose money by dealing with insignificant shit like this. We understand each other?”

Jimmy Bands nodded. “Aye, aye, Captain.” He saluted Phoenix and stared down at his two victims. “May Baby, shawty, call my cleanup crew. Let's knock this shit out so we can get back to the money.” He side-eyed Phoenix. “Next time, give me the benefit of the doubt, Blood. Shit should never have to come to dis.”

Phoenix smiled sinisterly. “When it comes to my money, shit like this happening is the least of what's gon’ take place. Trust me on that. Find a replacement. And you're all out of strikes. Later.” Phoenix nodded at his security detail, and they left the basement.

Jimmy Bands stood there for a long time, mugging the steps. “Bitch-ass nigga think it's sweet,” he grumbled.

May Baby eased over to him and stepped beside him. She laid her head on his shoulder and slid her arm around his waist. “That's okay, Jimmy, that nigga gon' be out of the picture real soon, and then Houston and Memphis will be yours, baby. There is only enough here for one king, and that king is you. Just wait on yo’ moment while we keep setting shit in place.”

“Yeah, boo, you're right. Fuck Phoenix. Dat nigga living on borrowed time.”

“And don't we both know it.” She hugged him tighter, kissed his cheek, then looked over the next tasks that needed cleaning up.

It was all a part of the game that the both of them were looking to master together.

Chapter 5
A year later

Natalia held out her hands as Phoenix Jr. stood up on wobbly legs. He sniffled and wiped tears from his eyes. Natalia squatted down and held out her arms even wider. "Come on, baby, you can do it, come to Mommy." Natalia's long, black, curly hair blew in the wind as the sun reflected off of her forehead.

Phoenix Jr. took another step forward, and then another. He held his hands out and wiped the final tears from his eyes as he made his way toward his mother. He got halfway to her and fell back on his Pamper. He burst into tears.

Natalia rushed to his side, ready to pick him up. "Aw, baby, don't cry. Mama got you."

Before she could pick him up, Taurus stepped out of the shadows of the backyard. "Leave him, Natalia!"

Natalia jumped and stopped as soon as the command left his lips. A chill ran down her spine. She purposely refused to look over at him. Instead, she kept her eyes on her son. "Daddy, constantly allowing him to fall without comforting him isn't helping him to learn anything other than the fact that it may seem that there is a lack of love for him in this home."

Taurus slid his Gucci shades from his face and tucked the glasses inside his shirt pocket. He directed Natalia to stop and to get away. She smacked her lips and followed his directive. Taurus knelt down and pulled up his pants leg a bit. He looked directly at Phoenix Jr. "Phoenix, grandson, look at me."

The child huffed and puffed, then stopped and looked over at his grandfather. He stuck his forefinger in his mouth and chewed on the nail, afraid.

"Phoenix, get up and walk to me. Now, and no more crying. Get up." The wind caused Taurus's shirt to flutter, along with his pants.

Junior stood up and steadied himself on his legs. He blinked and tears came down his cheeks. “Mommy! Mommy, I scared!”

“Aw, baby.” Natalia got ready to rush to his side again.

Taurus eyed her angrily. She stopped in her tracks and backed up. He moved only slightly closer to his grandson. “Phoenix, come to me now, or Pa Pa gon' spank that li'l butt. Now come!”

“Daddy, not so mean. He's struggling.”

“Natalia, quiet. Phoenix, come,” Taurus ordered.

“Whatever, man.” She smacked her lips and folded her arms.

Taurus watched Junior take a step forward. He stopped and began to cry. He looked up toward Natalia and sat back on his Pamper. Taurus stood up. “That's it. Go in the house, Natalia - now.”

“But Daddy, I didn't do nothing,” she whined.

“The sight of you is making my grandson weaker. When he sees you, he sees himself being rescued. He needs for you as his crutch to be nonexistent. Take yo’ butt in the house and leave me with him. Do it.”

“But Daddy, can I at least kiss him first?” She felt sick to her stomach and prayed that Taurus wouldn't be too hard on her son. Though he was eighteen months old, he often had trouble with the feat of walking. She didn't personally think it was a major problem, but after doing a bit of research, she found that Junior was a bit delayed, and this sometimes worried her. She did find that he was very intelligent and advanced in all other areas of his early childhood development.

“Natalia, don't make me say it again.” He pointed toward the house and waited until she disappeared inside after taking one final glance at Junior. As soon as she was out of sight, Taurus rushed over to Junior and picked him up. He leaned into his ear. "Now you listen to me, grandson. You are a Stevens. You come from a bloodline of kings. You are not weak. You are strong, and there is nothing that you can't have or conquer. You are going to get up and walk right now, or you are going to get a butt whipping. Now get up and do it." He backed away a safe distance and held his arms out.

Junior stood and cried for a second, and then he bit into his bottom lip. His head full of curly hair shone in the sunlight. He huffed and took a deep breath, then he swallowed his spit and took a step forward. He stopped, unsure. He looked around for Natalia. "Mama! Mom-MA!" He looked around again.

Taurus slapped his hands together and frowned. He pulled his belt off. "Phoenix, come to me, or I am going to come to you with this. Now come on!"

Junior began to cry again. He took a step forward, and then another. His legs wobbled. He nearly fell, but caught his balance.

Taurus slapped the belt on the ground. "Come! Now!"

In fear of getting a whipping, Junior slowly stepped one foot in front of the other until he was walking. He held his little arms out reaching for Taurus. "Pa Pa."

Taurus backed up further and further. He wanted to smile, but he remained chaste. He kept his face blank and continued to order his grandson forward. "Come on, baby. There you go. Come to me. A little more. That's it." Taurus kept backing up until he made two full revolutions around the big backyard that had a twenty-five meter pool right in the center of it. By the time he was ready to make one final half round, Natalia could no longer contain herself. He watched his daughter throw open the patio door and rush into the backyard.

"Oh my God! I knew it! I knew it! I knew you could do it, baby!" She ran over and picked Junior up into the air, twirling him around, kissing all over him.

Taurus frowned. "You're making him weak. Stop all that damn kissing on that baby."

Natalia ignored him. "Daddy, I'm just proud of my son. He walked around the entire yard more than twice, and he didn't fall once. That's amazing. He deserves this love. Besides, love isn't a bad thing. Perhaps if you got some, you wouldn't be so bitter." She rolled her eyes and glared at him.

Taurus eyed her for a long time in silence. "Natalia, I'm not going to go there with you today. You're feisty, hard headed, and I'm not going to let you worry me. But I want to show you somethin'."

"Yeah? And what's that?"

Phoenix stepped into the doorway of the patio. He eyed the trio and maintained his silence. He took a sip from his bottled water and smiled. Father and daughter were always arguing about something. He felt that they were too much alike, and that was the problem.

"Put him down, back up, and tell him to walk to you," Taurus ordered.

"Why? We saw that he can. He doesn't have anything to prove to either of us." She hugged Junior again and kissed him.

"Natalia, please, baby, do like I say before I choke your defiant ass. Now go." Taurus felt his blood pressure rising.

"Fine." She placed Junior on his Jordans and backed up. "Come on, baby, come to Mama, I'm right here."

Junior took a step forward on shaky legs and fell. He sat there and began to cry. Natalia got ready to rush over and pick him up. Taurus grabbed her, preventing her from doing so.

"Daddy, what are you doing?" Natalia asked.

"Move, girl, and watch this." Taurus waited for her to once again retreat, and then he assumed the position that she was just in. He clapped his hands together. "Come, Phoenix, now, or get yo li'l butt whipped."

Junior looked over at his mother. "Mommy!"

"Ain't no Mommy! Come now, boy!" Taurus roared. "Get up and walk."

Phoenix Jr. stood up and began to walk as he'd done before with ease. Taurus backed up further and further until once again they had made a full revolution around the yard. At the conclusion, he stepped into Natalia's space. "He is of a royal bloodline. If you handle him with softness, his legs will not work. On the other hand, if you handle him with authority and treat him like a king-to-be he will respond. Nothing that comes from us is weak." He kissed her on the cheek and walked into the house.

Phoenix stepped outside and walked over to Natalia. "Say, shawty, yo' Pops might be stuck in his ways and all dat shit, but dat nigga know what he talking 'bout. We gotta let him get Junior right. You see how intelligently he responds when yo' old man in the driver's seat, don't you?"

Junior walked to Natalia's legs and hugged them. He began to cry. "Mommy. Up-up."

Natalia placed a tuft of hair behind her ear. "Phoenix, this is your son. You are his father. My father should not have to step in and do your job. You should understand our son just as much as he does, so don't give me no shit."

Phoenix held up his hand. "Whoa, whoa, shawty. How dis turn around on me? I was just stating a fact."

"Nawl, you was just getting on my nerves." She rolled her eyes and scooped Junior into the air. "It seems like you pay close attention to Shanté, and barely any to our son. I understand that she is older now and clingy to you, but split the difference and get on board with your junior, you got me?" Natalia was irritated with Taurus and couldn't help releasing her anger and frustrations out on Phoenix. He was an easy target. She didn't feel like beefing with her father.

Phoenix sucked his teeth and rubbed his chin. "Shawty, you right. I'ma get more involved. Just let me know what you need from me?"

"To love him like you love Shanté. This is our son, and he is struggling wit' walking. That should be concerning to you." She adjusted Junior on her hip and kissed his cheek.

"Awright, I got him. You want me to work wit' him right now?" Phoenix reached for his son.

Natalia shook her head. "Nawl, I got him. You need to go in there and holler at my dad about the major invasion down in Texas. Y'all gon' need to get on the same page in order to pull it off. Rivera just endorsed the Bread Gang, and Bagg is their king. His ties run all through Memphis and back to the A. Not saying that I am worried, but this war is a cause for concern, that's all I'm thinking. So you go take care of that, and I'll take care of him - for now. But more help from you will be amazing."

Phoenix pulled her to him and kissed her lips. "I got you, boo. You already know that we are in this together."

"Yeah, we better be, or else I'ma take yo' ass out the game." She kissed his lips again and walked away from him.

As she was going into the mansion, Shanté came out with a bottle of suntan lotion in one hand and a beach towel in the other. Her Burberry one piece fit her snugly. She smiled at Natalia and kept walking up and into Phoenix's arms. "Hey Daddy." She stepped on her tippy toes and kissed his lips.

Phoenix returned her kiss and hugged her body. "Hey baby, what you up to?"

"I just wanted to get some sunlight since I can't go anywhere because of this daggone Coronavirus. I already know that once all of y'all get packed into the mansion that it's about to be a bunch or arguing and stuff, so I'm getting my space, peace, and tranquility right now. Uncle Taurus said that his daughter Jahliyah is coming into town this week to see him. Do you know her?"

"A li'l bit. From what I can remember, she cool people. Why, are you worried about her coming?"

"I just know that Natalia gets really jealous when it comes to other women being around you. I don't want y'all fighting over nothing. That makes me miserable. Plus, I don't want you to get so cool wit' Taurus's daughter that she takes up all of your attention and time. I need you too, Daddy." She laid her head on his shoulder.

"I know you do, li'l baby. Don't worry, Daddy ain't gon' let nobody take yo place. You are my number one, baby. I love you the most." He kissed her forehead.

Shanté smiled. "Thank you for saying that, Daddy. I needed to hear it." She hugged him and walked over to her lounge chair and laid back, proceeding to rub the suntan lotion into her caramel skin. "Daddy, before you go, can you get my back?" She lowered her straps just a tad and turned away from him.

Phoenix looked toward the mansion and back to Shanté. Natalia's last words about his and Shanté's close relationship played over in his head. "Baby, you sure you need my help?"

Shanté laughed. "Yeah, Daddy, here." She held the bottle out to him.

Phoenix took the bottle of lotion and took a final glance toward the mansion. There stood Natalia in the middle of the patio doorway with a curious eyebrow raised. Phoenix jumped. He cleared his throat and looked down at Shanté's exposed shoulders and upper back. “Say, li'l mama, you already know how jealous Natalia be getting because of how close you and I are, so Daddy gon' pass on this one because she is standing right there in the doorway with that crazy look on her face.”

Shanté turned to see what Phoenix was talking about. She and Natalia locked eyes. She sighed. “Dang, I just wish I could have my daddy all to myself.” She rolled her eyes at Natalia and took the bottle from Phoenix. “I love you, Daddy. I guess I'll talk to you later.” She pulled her straps in place and stretched out on her lounge chair.

Phoenix hung his head and shook it. “Damn, man.” When he looked over to locate Natalia, she was gone. He took one final glance at Shanté sprawled out on the lounge chair before he disappeared into the mansion with his mind racing a million miles a second.

Chapter 6

It was three o'clock in the afternoon on a bright and sunny Wednesday when Jimmy Bands slammed a fifty round clip into his F&N and cocked it. He pulled the red bandana over his face and looked over his shoulder to make sure that his four shooters had loaded up their weapons, and were ready to follow behind him. All throughout the Mercedes Benz van were the sounds of magazines being slammed into weapons before they were cocked and ready to blow. The interior's scent was heavy Kush and codeine. Jimmy Bands was high as gas prices, and his eyes were lower than an ugly nigga's self-esteem.

"Say, mane, y'all already know how dese Bread Gang niggas get down. They shiesty, and they ain't got no ma'fuckin' loyalty. It was one thang when they wanted to kick that dumb shit over in Memphis, but now they venturing over to Harris County where the Duffle Bag Cartel runs shit. We gon' go in dis bitch and knock out as many brains as possible. I don't give a fuck if it's a nigga's or a bitch's. We gon' handle dis li'l bidness and then move into this building after the heat dies down. You muthafuckas feeling me right now, Blood?"

Rondo, a skinny, light-skinned, sixteen-year-old shooter with a bunch of loose screws and freckles all over his face, laughed. "Hell yeah, Joe. Can't wait to handle dese niggas. They music ain't even all dat. They ain't got shit on my li'l potnas, and 'sides, I feel like they need to be knocked down a few pegs." He rubbed the side of his Draco and kissed the black barrel.

Phoenix had given Jimmy Bands the go ahead to annihilate the ten men that currently sat inside of the barbershop. The shop was a front for them to sell large potent quantities of Sinaloa heroin that was imported by Rivera straight into the heart of the slums of Memphis and Harris County. Both sections were heavily-ridden and dominated by the Duffle Bag Cartel, and Phoenix refused to share his wealth or his turf.

Jimmy Bands sucked his good teeth. "Well, seeing as we understand each other, let's get this shit cracking. Ma'fuckas follow my lead, and no remorse. If you freeze, I'm squeezing on you right where you stand. Let's roll." He pulled his shirt over his guns and allowed the driver to pull the van to the corner of the block where BGE Barbershop was located. Jimmy Bands hopped out of the van and pulled his hood over his head. His goons followed him and did the same thing. They made sure that they stayed a safe distance behind so that they could survey the area.

The street was almost vacant, with the exception of a few women coming out of the beauty salon that was directly across the street from the Barbershop. BGE not only had a barbershop for the men, but they owned a hair salon right across from the shop that catered to the women. Jimmy Bands thought about running in there and dropping as many bodies as he could just to make a statement, but decided against it for this day, as too many murders in one afternoon caused the Feds to get involved. He could handle the local authorities, but the Feds was another story.

He strolled past the fruit stand that was twenty feet away from the barbershop. A small Mexican woman tried her best to promote her fresh watermelons and cantaloupes. Jimmy Bands ignored her and pulled his hood tauter as he approached the entrance to the door of his targets. He grabbed the door handle and pulled it outward. A bell sounded to announce that a new customer had arrived in the shop. All of the patrons turned to look at him. As he was coming in, there was a female with a Coronavirus mask across her face coming out of the shop after having her son's hair cut. She nodded at Jimmy

Bands and squeezed past him and then his crew that smelled like worn cologne, alcohol, and Kush. Jimmy Bands thought about pulling her back inside of the shop and killing her and her kid along with everybody else, but then Sosa, one of the Bread Gang enemies, and him made eye contact.

Before Jimmy Bands could reach for his F&N, Sosa pushed the person's hair that he was cutting forward and slipped his hand into the back of the seat, removing a Glock Nineteen. It was already cocked. He upped it and began firing while running toward the back door of the shop. “It’s a hit, Joe! It's a hit!” he hollered at the top of his lungs.

Boom! Boom! Boom!

Whoom! Whoom! Whom! Whoom!

Jimmy Bands ran toward him, blowing back to back. His first three bullets missed, and his fourth caught Sosa in the chest and knocked him through the back door. Sosa hollered out in pain, then jumped up and took off running, feeling like his ribs were breaking with each stride that he took down the back alley. Jimmy Bands was about to follow suit when three shots came his way. He fell to the ground of the barbershop, shooting at the two BGE females that had run from across the street from the salon to assist their fellow comrades. They busted fully automatic Tech Nines with the intent to slay him and his crew. All around the shop, guns were being let off. A thick cloud of gray smoke emitted into the air and filled the room.

Jimmy Bands got up to his knee and started to bust with precision. He aimed at one target at a time and pulled his trigger. The bullets zipped out of his gun and flew across the room, hitting one mark after the next. His slugs knocked half of a female's head off. She fell to her knees with her finger on the trigger of her weapon before falling to her death. Jimmy Bands jumped up. He fired two more rounds and connected with the second female from across the street. His bullet punched a hole through her neck and killed her before she could fall to her knees.

His troops fired and fired. Nine out of the ten men that they'd come to slay were deceased and riddled with bullets. Outside, the street was cluttered with people fleeing to their cars to get away from the gruesome scene inside of the shop. They jumped inside of their whips and screeched away from the curb at full speed.

"Let's get the fuck out of here, now!" Jimmy Bands ordered.

They ran out of the back door of the shop and were met by his young driver. Jimmy Bands jumped inside of the passenger's seat, sinking to the floor. The side of the van was opened, and his crew rushed inside and laid on the floor out of sight with their guns still smoking. By the time the police rolled on to the scene where the multiple murders had taken place, Jimmy Bands and his crew were already ten miles away, and Jimmy was on the phone with Phoenix relaying that the mission was complete in such a way that only the two of them knew what they were talking about.

***

Natalia sat at her vanity table brushing her curly hair. She'd just gotten Junior to sleep, and she was exhausted. She stroked her hair fifty more times before she set the brush on the table and looked into the mirror at her reflection. She stared long and hard before she took a deep breath and sighed. "Where are the years going?" She asked this question out loud and in Russian.

Phoenix eased into the room. He pulled his shirt off and tossed it onto the bed. "Baby, you in hurr talking to yourself?" he asked in Russian.

Natalia nodded. "Yeah, not so much as myself, but more out loud than anything. I see your Russian is getting better."

"I do what I do." Phoenix walked over to her and tried to pull her up.

"Phoenix, come on now, I'm so tired that I can't even think straight." She stood up and faced him reluctantly.

Phoenix brushed her hair behind her earlobes and kissed her lips. "Say, shawty, over the last few months, we ain't kicked it the way we usually do. I feel like a major part of us is missing, and I don't like it."

Natalia batted her long eyelashes and smiled. "Wow, you sound like the woman right now."

Phoenix released her. "I'm good." He started to walk away, but she grabbed him.

"Phoenix, chill, man, I was just messing with you. Damn, why is it okay for you to mess with me, but when it comes to me toying with you it's hard for you to take it?"

"It ain't hard for me to take, but damn. Shawty, when we gon' fuck again? Shit been real weird ever since Junior came out of that womb. You already know I'm used to waxing that shit on a daily basis. What's good?" He slipped his arms around her waist and gripped her ass. It felt fluffier and rounder. This feeling caused his dick to stiffen. He pulled her closer to him.

Natalia tried to break away. "Boy, the baby ain't got nothing to do wit' it. How are we going to get down with my father roaming around the house? I don't want him hearing me moaning and all of that. Besides, we still ain't even asked him how he feels about you and I having a baby together and living under the same roof. We still are family. Did you forget that?"

"Shawty, did you forget how good this Russian and Black pussy is? I really don't give a fuck how Taurus feel about me and you. Shid, he know he got a bad-ass daughter, all thick and shit. On everythang, I done caught that nigga looking at yo' ass on more than one occasion."

"Phoenix." She slapped him on the shoulder.

"I'm serious too. I mean, dat nigga was all up in yo' shit like he couldn't believe how bad you were neither. If anything, he understand why I had to fuck wit' you on that level. Besides, if that nigga'll fuck his mother, you already know not only do he not give a fuck about what we doing, but yo' li'l ass ain't off limits neither." He kissed her neck and scraped at the veins with his teeth. "Knowing how crazy you are about this blood on blood shit, it'll probably drive you crazy imagining yo' Pops fucking this fat-ass booty." He pulled her gown up slowly and felt between her thighs. Her pussy was soaking wet. He sucked on her neck.

"Mmm, shut up, Phoenix. My daddy ain't even thinking about no shit like that. I'm his li'l girl, and he sees me as his baby."

"Yeah, well I got news for you, Natalia: you really ain't no baby no more. Not with all this ass, and these perfect-ass titties. Ain't no way I'd be able to keep my hands off of you. I wouldn't give a fuck what you were to me. That Stevens blood runs deep within my veins, just like it does yours." He slipped his middle finger into her pussy and it sucked it inside of her hungrily.

Natalia's nipples felt like they were going to pop off of her chest. Her breathing became ragged. She imagined Taurus coming at her the wrong way and it both angered and then excited her. She shook the thoughts out of her mind and diagnosed them as wrong. She removed her pussy from off of Phoenix's finger and felt her juices slide down her inner thighs. "Phoenix, I ain't fucking wit' you right now. I'm too tired, and you got my head spinning in the wrong direction.

My daddy ain't looking at me like that. I know him better than you think." She turned to walk away.

Phoenix snatched her up and forced her face first into the wall. He slipped his hand back under her nightgown and found her leaking pussy. He separated the lips and drove two fingers into her. "Me and Taurus got the same blood. If you drive me crazy, you better believe that you drive him crazy too." He bit into her neck. "You don't see what I see. I done caught him peeping you with hunger in his eyes. He wanna fuck and finesse this pussy. Imagine that shit, boo. Close yo' eyes and imagine yo' Pops tearing this ass up." He increased his fingerings.

"Unh! Unh! Unh!" Natalia laid her face sideways on the wall with her mouth wide open. "Stop, Phoenix. Stop, Phoenix, you're fuckin' up my head. I ain't on that taboo shit no more. I got a baby now."

"Yeah? So that's why you ain't been trying to fuck yo' baby daddy? What, 'cause we blood?" He unbuckled his Ferragamo belt and pulled his pants down. His dick sprang up hard and ready for action. He kicked her feet apart and searched for her entrance with his big dick head. "You finna give me this pussy, right now. You belong to me. You're my blood." He sank into her heat and pushed forward.

"Unnnnnnn, fuck!" she screamed. She placed her palms on the wall as Phoenix took a hold of her long hair, forcing her to arch her back. "Shit!"

Phoenix slapped her ass hard and fucked her with hard, long strokes that caused her ass to vibrate and jiggle. He took a hold of her hips. "Uhhhh. Uhhhh. Cuz, this that good-ass pussy. Awww, you so wet. You so ma'fuckin' wet." He slipped his hand between her thighs and diddled her clitoris.

A jolt of sexual energy shot up through Natalia. She screeched and moaned out loud, praying that Taurus could not hear her. Her long tongue ran all over her juicy lips. She imagined Taurus busting into the room and catching Phoenix screwing her in the fashion that he was and it was enough to make her shiver and shake uncontrollably. "Awwww, shit, baby." She came.

Phoenix pulled out and pushed her to the floor. He got her to the carpet and dove back inside of her, where he began to pound her out at full speed as hard as he could. "You my bitch. You belong to dis family. You a Stevens. Dat pussy belongs to us. Even if Taurus wanna fuck." He dug deeper.

"Awwww, shut up. Shut up, oooh, fuck! I'm cumming again." She pulled him down to her and stuck her nails in his back.

Phoenix felt her cumming underneath him and it drove him overboard. He squeezed her titties together, eyed the inch long light brown nipples, and came deep inside of her. He pulled out and came all over her stomach and titties. "Yeah, boo, yeah, oooh shit, yeah." He pumped his dick and came some more. He leaned down and kissed all over her lips, rubbing her jerking pussy mound the entire time.

Natalia laid on her back with her thick thighs wide open. Her pussy was leaking like never before. She looked into Phoenix's eyes. "Uh, uh, uh, boy, you ain't no good."

"And knowing that is half the battle. I love our blood. Fuck the world." He meant that.

Taurus had been walking past their bedroom when he'd heard his name. This prompted him to stop and to see what they were talking about. Before he knew it, he was watching the entire scene unfold before him. He eased away from the door with a variety of mixed emotions. One thing was for sure was that the sin factor of his bloodline ran deep.

Chapter 7

Taurus pulled his Alexander Wang suit coat closed as he made his way across the rooftop of Miami Pharmaceuticals. The side of the helicopter's door slid open and he stepped inside of it. Phoenix sat in the caramel leather seat directly in front of the door, puffing on a stuffed OG Kush blunt with his eyes low and a Duffle bag filled with a half a million dollars in cash. Taurus pulled the chopper's door closed behind him, and fastened his seat belt.

Phoenix handed him the Duffle bag. “Here you go, Unc. That's five hundred thousand dollars in cash in about twelve hours. I been having a few of my traps push that new yellow Mollie you created, and that shit hitting harder than the MLB. Phoenix took a puff off of his blunt and smiled. Behind them were two armed guards. One was Jimmy Bands, and the other was an old school cat named Rocket from back in the times of Taurus's old running days. Rocket was six feet even, two hundred pounds, and cold-hearted. His loyalty was to Taurus, and only Taurus.

Taurus took the bag off of his lap and set it on the floor of the helicopter. “That's good to know, nephew. That was just a sample shipment. The new shit that's coming in is guaranteed to blow Harris County wide open, and the homeland as well. I say within the next two weeks, you should be seeing more money than you ever have in your entire life. You gotta be ready for the haters to rear their ugly heads even more than they had before.”

Phoenix laughed. “Last thang I'm worried about is a ma’fuckin’ hater. I been getting hated on ever since I broke the threshold of a hundred thousand dollars. We got plans for haters. Ain't that right, Jimmy baby?” Phoenix looked back at Jimmy Bands.

"You know dat. This Duffle Bag all day right here, Shawty. Ma'fuckas want the smoke, it won't cost them a dime." Jimmy Bands said this with pride.

Taurus looked back at him and frowned. "You thank that pistol that you carrying on yo' waist gon' be able to stop everybody that's about to come out of the woodwork at you boys' heads?"

Jimmy shrugged his shoulders. "Say, mane, I don't know, but you damn sho' better believe that I'ma try and knock off every nigga's head that even thank shit sweet. If I don't get 'em all at once, you better believe that their names will be added to the short list." He laughed and nodded whut up to Phoenix. Phoenix diverted his eyes because he knew that Taurus was about to pour into his ass.

Taurus shook his head. "Li'l nigga, that gun only holds a maximum of fifty shots. Then you gotta take the time to load it up again. That means that you will be vulnerable. You have to sleep. That means that you will be vulnerable. In order for a made nigga to really survive in the game, you must have a team of loyal savages around you at all times. This also makes you vulnerable." Taurus paused and looked over to Phoenix. Phoenix was all ears, and silent. "You see, what you li'l brothers have to understand is that the more blood you shed, the less money you'll be able to make and the shorter your run will be at the top of the totem pole - assuming you make it that far. Murder and guns are necessary, but they must be strategic."

Phoenix side-eyed Taurus. "Wait a minute now, Unc, you a ma'fuckin' legend in the slums. You been bussing niggas' heads ever since the early thousands. You mean to tell me that every nigga you ever chopped was for a strategic reason?"

Taurus shook his head. "Once upon a time, I was just as naïve and angry as you li'l homies, but then I reached that certain level in the game that most ma'fuckas only dream of, and those real haters came for my life in a major way. That's when I had to get smarter, and that's when the game took on a new ambiance for me mentally and psychologically."

"Fuck level is dat? Ma'fuckas already eating like it's a buffet around dis bitch. We crush niggas on a regular, and ain't no ma'fucka came at us yet that ain't been put down. So yeah, my nigga, fuck level is you really talking 'bout?" Jimmy Bands wanted to know.

"Say, Blood, watch how you talking to my people. That's my uncle, and not only is he that, but he is a legend in our slums. Honor him like them niggas from the A honor Meech."

Rocket chimed in. "Meech ain't got shit on Taurus. Taurus is the nigga that supplied him and got those Quality Control niggas off the ground. Y'all gotta do ya research before you get to capping off." He glanced at Jimmy Bands with his trigger finger itching.

"Unc, you supplied Meech? Damn, you were that heavy in the game?" Phoenix was impressed.

Taurus ignored his question and instead he looked over at Jimmy Bands. "Say, li'l brother, what's the most money you've ever seen in yo' life?"

The helicopter experienced a bit of turbulence. It shook for a second and began to sail normally after a moment.

"I don't thank all dat's important, Blood. I know that ever since I been running under that fool Phoenix, I ain't been broke, and these designer jeans have been fitting me tight. I got two cribs and three whips, mo' bitches than a new doggy litter, and niggas ain't fuckin' wit' my bidness. Whatever level comes next, on bro, I'm stepping up. That's what dat is right thurr, homeboy." Jimmy's heart began to beat faster. Who was Taurus to check his bag count? He felt disrespected. He didn't give a fuck about Taurus's legendary status.

Taurus nodded. "Awright den, li'l homie, you got it. I'ma let my nephew continue to guide you, and I'ma fall back. My parting words are simply this. You'll know when you reached that next level because everybody who you thought were your friends will become your foes, and those real haters that I speak of will be to see you." Taurus turned back around and sat in his seat. He licked an old school Garcia Vega that was stuffed with Purple Haze and sparked it.

Phoenix was lost in thought. He wondered if he was anywhere near that status. He had six million tucked away in an offshore account and two million in cash put up in a few safes. His net worth in the streets was currently two million, so that gave him a grand total of ten million even. He couldn't think of any real enemies other than the ones that he created for himself, and because he couldn't he felt that he was lacking a need to level up. He needed to bust a series of moves to get more grounding. He was sure that after he crushed the Bread Gang and conquered Rivera, the drug market would open up for him and he would be right where he needed to be. His current goal was to chase and capture a total of twenty million.

***

That night, Natalia strolled into Taurus's room just as he pulled his bulletproof vest off of his chest. He dropped it on the bed, then pulled two twin .44 Magnums out of his waistband and had them cocked and aimed at her before she could fully step into the room.

Natalia stopped in her tracks and held up her hands. "Daddy, it's just me. What are you doing?"

Taurus's chest heaved up and down. He was in a murderous zone for a moment longer, and then he slowly came out of it. Natalia's physical features came into view. He lowered his weapons and exhaled. “Damn, baby, you gotta announce yourself.” He laid the guns on the dresser and lowered his head. His body was ripped with muscles, and heavily tatted. He had a hint of a stomach, but even it was packed with abs.

“I'm sorry, Daddy.” Natalia slipped beside him and ran her hand over his muscular back. She cruised over him until her hands landed on his chest. He turned around to face her. She looked up into his eyes. Her arms went around his neck as she continued to gaze into his honey brown-colored eyes. “Daddy, we need to talk. I think it's time you tell what's going on with you, and who you're running from.”

“Running?” Taurus stepped out of her embrace. “I ain't never ran from nobody in my entire life. Those that run are cowards. Your father ain't got that coward shit in him.”

Natalia stood a safe distance from him for a while. His back was to her. Then she went to him and hugged his massive back. She kissed it. “Daddy, I'm not saying that you are afraid of anybody, but I can sense with my womanly intuition that something is not right with you. I am your little girl. I know we just met not too long ago, but I love you, and I need to know what we are up against. I need to understand you as my father, and as the man that I have always yearned to meet. Your blood runs deep in my veins.” She kissed his back again, and rubbed around to his swollen chest that had a picture of Princess tatted on one side and Blaze on the other. Both were the loves of his life, but Princess more so than Blaze. Both had been murdered because of a forbidden love - a forbidden love that had cost him so much.

Taurus turned around and took hold of Natalia. He rubbed her face with his thumbs. “My job is to protect you, and to keep you as far away from my affairs as possible. The less you know, the better.”

Natalia frowned and dropped her hands to her sides before she balled them into fists. “I don't need you trying to protect me from anything or anyone, especially if they are set out to hurt you, or anybody that is under this roof.” She stepped into his face. “Are you in danger? And more importantly, because of your affairs, am I, Junior, or Phoenix in trouble?”

Taurus looked down on her for a few seconds before a slight dimpled smile came across his face. He stroked her soft cheek. “When your face turns to a ball of anger, you look just like my mother. Her features run rampant through you.” He continued to rub her cheek.

Natalia flared her nostrils. She mugged him for a full thirty seconds, then softened. She took a hold of his hand and forced it to open so that her face was resting in the palm of it. “Daddy, I love you so much. I am concerned for you, and I don't like the fact that you treat me as if I am a defenseless little girl. I am your daughter, a warrior in my heart and by blood. I am not like most feeble-minded women. I am a gladiator, and I have an army of assassins that are loyal to me. This woman that you see before you is not weak, but powerful.”

Taurus took her small, makeup-less face into his big hands and placed his forehead against hers. “Baby, I don't care how tough you are, or how many assassins you have running behind you. If they don't have our blood, then you shouldn't trust them, and even if they do, you shouldn't. When it comes to my affairs, your father is more than capable of conquering them when the time is right. Are you more worried because I have chosen to take up your guest room for a season or two?” He studied her.

Natalia shook her head. “Never, Daddy. Having you here has been the greatest gift of my life, if I'm being quite honest. I love waking up and knowing that my father is just down the hall. It makes me feel secure and loved." She stepped on her tippy toes and wrapped her arms around his neck.

Taurus took a hold of her small waist. His face sank into the crux of her neck before he hugged her frame to him. "I promise, baby, that when the time is right for me to explain everything to you, then I will. Until then, I just need for you to trust me and to cherish the moments that we have together. Life is precious."

Natalia's heart sank. Immediately she started to imagine the negative possibilities of his statement. She swallowed the lump in her throat and felt sick. "Daddy, I don't know what that means, and I don't want to. All I know is that I love you, and I have always yearned for you. Now that you're here, I will die before I let you go." She gave him a quick peck on the lips, then she hugged him with an emotional bond that even he didn't understand as of yet.

Taurus became weary. He needed to get things in order. He didn't like the thought of being on borrowed time. He had to master his situation and come out as he always had: on top.

"I love you, li'l baby, and Daddy promises you that he got this."

He picked her up, and she wrapped her legs around him. He held her just like that for the next few minutes before they parted ways for the night, both with heavy, stressed hearts.

Chapter 8

"Say, mane, can't no ma'fucka tell us we ain't getting money. Can't no nigga out here check a bag like we checking, Jimmy. I'm a young nigga, sixteen, and I got a hunnit G's in my lap to fuck off like this shit light. I'll sweat somethin' over you, my nigga, that's on bro n'em grave. Nigga fuck wit' Jimmy Bands, and Rondo gon' knock his dick in the dirt." Rondo said this as he adjusted the duffle bag stuffed with a hundred thousand dollars' worth of cash in his lap. His F&N lay on top of it with a red beam attached to it.

Jimmy Bands glanced over at him and smiled. He eased his foot off the pedal of his brand new cherry red Porsche truck. He had the custom top dropped, and the sun reflected off of peanut butter soft leather seats that had the Gucci logo stitched into them, along with his name on the seats. "I'm 'bout that Almighty dolla, li'l bruh. Dese niggas rolling around fucked up and blaming the Coronavirus. Ma'fuckas acting like they can't get no money because of this virus. Mane, that's malarkey. The Cartel been getting ten times more money because of this pandemic. There is always another move, and it's for bosses to make them, and bums to complain about something or someone knocking them down a few pegs. Fuck a bum, Blood, straight up." He cruised past a group of scantily-clad females that were sitting on a porch in front of a rundown house. He beeped the horn and the females jumped up, thirsty for him to stop. "Nawl, bitches." He laughed. "Hoes always looking for a savior. I bet every last one of dem bitches got at least two baby daddies."

"Yeah, but dis Memphis, my nigga. Everybody fucking everybody. I bet out of those six hoes that at least two of dem share the same baby daddy."

Rondo placed his hand around one of his guns as they drove past a crowd of known stick-up kids. He mugged them and pulled up his red bandana over his nose to let them know what it was. In Memphis, when a shooter pulled his rag over his face, that meant that he was ready to murder something.

The two shooters in the back seat of Jimmy Bands' Porsche cocked their guns and mugged the stick-up kids. Jimmy Bands pulled his red bandana over his face and glared at them. As he slowly came to a halt at the stop sign where five more of them were gathered, he pulled a Tech on his lap and cocked it.

Three of the stick-up kids stepped into the middle of the street with blue 3M masks on their faces. One, a heavyset light-skinned man named Skully, held out his hand to stop Jimmy Bands from pulling off of the street. Jimmy slowed the whip and threw it in park, fearless. He jumped out of it, and two blunts fell off of his lap. Rondo hopped out as well.

"Say , mane, fuck you goofy-ass niggas hopping in da middle of da street fo'? Seems to me you suckas looking to get blown down," Jimmy snapped clutching his Tech.

Rondo never took his eyes off of Skully. He tightened his grip on both of his weapons and lowered his eyes. "Mane, on everythang I love, if you fuck niggas thank it's sweet 'cause we seeing cheddar, you bitches 'bout to see what it really is." Chills came over his body. He yearned to murder something.

Skully held up his hand. "Say, Jimmy, we ain't on shit wit' you, cuz, just following orders from Gunnah. Gunnah said don't nobody roll through the Mound no more that ain't living here. Technically, we supposed to be confiscating yo' whip and stripping you niggas."

Jimmy Bands aimed his Tech at him. "Try anythang like that, and I'll blow yo' shit back so fast that yo' homeboy standing next to you will have two to his face before you hit the ground. You niggas know what it is." Jimmy Bands growled and clenched his gold teeth.

Skully shook his head. "Nawl, nigga, shit ain't sweet in dis direction neither." Fifteen jack boys came and stood behind him with their revolvers and handguns tucked into their waistbands. They were ready to move at Skully's urging. "All I'm saying is dat Gunnah calling the shots fo' the Mound now. He got a stupid plug from back East, and he ain't trying to hear that Duffle Bag Cartel shit no more. Effective immediately, your kind ain't even welcome 'round dese parts no more. Y'all get dis last pass to roll through, but from here on out, you gotta get permission from Gunnah. Dat's what dat is right thurr."

Jimmy Bands felt offended. "Nigga, I was born and raised in Orange Mound. I smoked my first nigga right there." He pointed to the stop sign at the end of the block. "And I smoked my next three right on this strip. I got popped in Al's Liquor store parking lot, and again right on dis block. Bitch, I am Orange Mound. Can't no fuck nigga tell me different, mane, dat's what dat is. Y'all might as well smoke me right now."

A thirteen-year-old jack boy stepped in front of Skully with his .38 special cocked. "Shid, you ain't said nothin' but a word, cousin." He aimed his barrel at Jimmy, ready to splash him.

Rondo jumped in the way and smacked the gun out of the child's hand. He snatched him up and slammed his gun to his temple. "Y'all betta warn this fuck nigga. Dis ain't dat." He pushed him to the ground and kicked him as hard as he could in the ribs.

Skully and his team surrounded them. They were ready to gun them down. Skully helped his young hitta up and mugged Jimmy Bands. "Dis how you allowing for dis nigga to behave right now?"

"It is what it is. Dat's what loyalty looks like." He sucked his gold teeth. "Tell dat nigga Gunnah that he ain't running shit. Orange Mound still belongs to the Duffle Bag Cartel, and because Phoenix put me in charge of dis chapter, I'm ready to die 'bout dis turf. So when you see dat nigga, tell him I said if he ready to die for the Mound, den let's get it." Jimmy Bands held the Tech up against his shoulder. He was about to shoot into the air when he saw Gunnah walking down the strip of Orange Mound with twenty killas behind him. Jimmy Bands moved Skully out of the way, and made haste toward the man.

Gunnah was short, 5'5" tall, with long blond dreads that fell to his waist. He rocked all black with black and white Jordans, and an all-black Fendi Coronavirus mask that covered half of his face. His neck was flooded in gold jewelry, and he walked with a swag of confidence.

Jimmy stopped twelve feet away from him when he saw Gunnah's men up their weapons and aim at him. Jimmy ignored them. He'd grown up with most of Gunnah's posse and he felt that only a few of them were actual killas.

"Gunnah, fuck dis shit Skully over durr talking 'bout? Making it seem like we're rejected from the Mound. Who da fuck you thank you is, Blood?"

Gunnah pulled down his mask and smiled. He was handsome, yet sadistic. "My niggas gave you the order I gave them. Quite frankly, you s'posed to have brains leaking out of yo'; skull right now. It's a new day. Dis here is Sniper Gang. We plugged all da way from Memphis to Miami, boi, fuck wit' it." He stepped forward, and his shooters did as well.

It seemed as if the entire Orange Mound was out waiting to see what was about to happen. Females stood across the street, nosy and excited, while a bunch of dope boys that were soon to be hunted looked on from a distance. The sun was beaming high in the sky, and everybody outside was sweating profusely.

Jimmy Bands saw that he was outgunned and outmanned. He nodded his head. “Say, shawty, ever since you was a li'l nigga, we stole cars together and laid niggas on they face. Now you switching sides on the Cartel. For what? Nigga, for who?” Jimmy started to get angry.

“Fa me, nigga!” Gunnah stepped into his face. “Ain't nobody eat out of that Cartel but Phoenix and a chosen few others, but I ain't, so I don't give a fuck about none of you niggas. Dese are the forgotten ones. Dese are my people, and we eating like pigs around dis ma’fucka. It's Sniper Gang. Fuck wit’ it and get slumped, or keep it pushing and preserve yo’ life. Don't matter to me, homeboy.” He ran his tongue over his gold. “Either way, the Mound is mine. Fuck Duffle Bag!” He spit on the concrete.

Jimmy Bands was seconds away from blowing him down. He closed his eyes briefly and smiled while opening them. “Awright, homie, you got it. The Mound is Sniper Gang's.” He turned his back on Gunnah and proceeded to walk away. “Come on, Rondo.”

“So that's it You gon' simply roll over just like that? You ain't gon' even put up a fight? Man, you more bitch than I thought. I already know that you finna go and get that nigga Phoenix. Fuck him too. Tell cuz I said he can suck my dick, just like Skyy be doing.”

Jimmy Bands stopped in his tracks. He turned around. “Fuck you say ’bout my sister?”

Gunnah laughed. “Struck a nerve? Bitch, you heard me. Get the fuck out of my hood, or else.”

“Or else what, nigga?” Jimmy was ready for war.

“Shooters, commence on my command!” Gunnah hollered. His shooters took out their weapons if they weren't already out, and aimed them at the foursome. Gunnah laughed. “You got a minute to get out of the Mound, and that's without yo' Porsche. Swiss cheese dat bitch!"

Jimmy Band's henchmen ran away from the Porsche before the shooting started. Gunnah's hittas aimed and forced back to back, chopping up the Porsche. The females and children that were once across the street ran into every direction while bullets ate away at the paint and body of his Porsche. In less than fifteen seconds, the Porsche was mangled and smoking.

"Get the fuck out of the Mound, bitch! Sniper Gang!" Gunnah yelled and let off twenty shots into the air.

Jimmy Bands, Rondo, and their Shooters took off running, feeling emasculated.

Chapter 9

"Yo, baby, wake up. Wake up, li'l baby. Daddy wanna spend some time with you." Taurus nudged Natalia's shoulder lightly and waited for her to open her pretty eyes. "Come on, baby."

Natalia pulled the thick Burberry comforter back over her head. "Daddy, Junior had me up all night with his ear infection. I didn't get back from the hospital until three this morning. I'm tired. What time is it?"

Taurus looked over at the digital clock, which read one in the afternoon. "It's one, baby, get yo li'l butt up and come chill wit me." He frowned.

Natalia laid there for a second. She stretched her legs out and cracked her freshly-painted toes. She threw the blanket back to reveal her face to him. Her eyes had sleep within them. "Daddy, how is it so late and I feel so tired?"

Taurus leaned over the bed and proceeded to take the cold out of her eyes with his thumb and forefinger. He wiped them on a Kleenex and kissed her forehead. "It's good. We gon' chill for a few hours, and then we gon' let you rest while I go and handle some business. Now get up." He pulled the blanket down to her waist, exposing her breasts.

Natalia blushed, and pulled it back up. "Daddy."

Taurus jumped up and backed slowly from the bed. He turned away from her. "Damn, Natalia, I didn't know, baby, I swear I didn't."

She laid in the bed for a moment and laughed to herself. She was glad to see that Taurus was more embarrassed than she was. "Daddy, it's okay. After all, I'm yo' li'l girl. Get your mind out of the gutter." She slid out of the bed and stood up, shirtless. Her pink Victoria's Secret boy shorts were all up in her gap, exposing her lips. The back portion had both of her ass cheeks on display. "Daddy, are you okay?"

Taurus kept his back to her. He couldn't get the image of her breasts out of his mind. He shook his head. "Look, I'ma gon' head and let you get dressed. I'll meet you downstairs in twenty minutes. Junior is with Phoenix for the day, and he already knows that you and I will be spending some time together, so hurry up."

"Daddy?" Natalia called.

Taurus stopped in the doorway but didn't look back. "Yeah?"

"I'm not mad at you for seeing me. I mean, you are my father. I don't see what the big deal is."

"I'll meet you downstairs, baby. Hurry up." He left out the door and descended the steps.

Natalia felt as if something was ugly about her. She wondered if her body was unattractive now that Junior had come out of it. Taurus seemed as if he was more repulsed than embarrassed, and she didn't like that feeling. She thought about the impending arrival of Jahliyah, and wondered how she looked? She knew she was darker like Taurus, and probably favored him more. She wondered if they would have more of a connection because of the love Taurus had for Princess, and the lack of love he'd held for her mother Nastia? She also wondered if because Jahliyah was full Black if she would desire Taurus more than a father, and even go so far as to try and seduce him? If that was the case, then she already knew that she would lose her father for sure, and that would crush her. Suddenly she became angry.

She walked through the doorway of her bedroom. "Daddy!"

Taurus was in the midst of sitting on the couch and rolling a blunt. "Yeah, baby?"

"When is Jahliyah supposed to be coming again?"

"Two weeks."

Natalia cursed under her breath. "Did Phoenix say how long he was going to be taking care of Junior? Are we chilling for at least a full day or so?" She bit into her lowest lip, nervous. She had to lock down Taurus before Jahliyah had the chance.

"I told him that we'll be back in the morning. Why, are you thinking we should come back tonight or something?" Taurus sparked his blunt and inhaled a deep pull.

"Nawl, Daddy, I just wanted to make sure. I'll be down in a half hour." She stepped back into her bedroom with her jealousy getting the better of her and tried as best she could to clear her mind. She hadn't even met Jahliyah yet, and she didn't like her.

***

Taurus opened the passenger's door to his all-black McLaren and allowed Natalia to slip inside and on to the red leather seat. She sat and pulled her short Prada miniskirt down as far as she could, but her thighs were so thick that it almost looked like a failed attempt. She placed her Hermes bag on her lap as Taurus closed the door and walked around to the other side.

"Baby, I know that ever since I popped back up on the scene that I ain't been nothing but a closed book, but I'm hoping that by the end of this li'l daddy and daughter kicking it time, you and I have a broader understanding of everything. Cool?" He said this as he settled behind the wheel and started the engine.

"That's cool, Daddy. I just don't want to be left in the dark. I love you enough to love you through whatever you got going on, and I need for you to know that I got your back one hundred percent. You're the only parent that I have walking this earth."

Taurus pulled down the long driveway and out of the South Beach gated community. The mansion where they resided had at one point in time belonged to LeBron James. Whenever Taurus walked through it, he couldn't help but to remind himself of that.

"Well, baby, the first thing I want us to be able to do is during this whole time, I want for us to be completely honest with one another, and I want for us to be able to ask each other anything that we really want to know. I am an open book to you, and I want for you to be the same with me." He pulled onto the highway just as the sun broke through the clouds to shine brightly. Miami beamed and smelled like the ocean. To Taurus, Miami was one of the most beautiful cities on earth, but within the pit of his stomach, he missed Memphis.

"That's cool with me, Daddy. I feel like we should have come under this banner a long time ago. The first thing I wanna know, and you need to be honest with me… Will you?" She lowered the window and her long hair began to fly out of it.

"Of course I will. Shoot."

"I need to know if you love Jahliyah more than me, and if so, why?" She frowned and crossed her arms.

Taurus raised his right eyebrow. "Really, that's your first question?"

She nodded. "Sho' is. Please answer that for me."

Taurus shook his head. "No, I don't. I love the both of you the same. What would make you ask me that question?"

"Because it was really heavy on my heart, and I know damn well that no parent can possibly love their children the exact same way. It sounds good, but is it really the truth though?" She shrugged her shoulders. "The reason I ask this is because you were in love with her mother, and you didn't give two fucks about mine, excuse my French. I could see myself loving the child of the man I loved the most over just some drive-by kid that happened on accident. Sometimes I just wonder, how much do you really care about me?"

Taurus ran his hand over his deep waves and kept rolling. He felt a lump form in his throat. "Baby, I love you because you are my daughter, and you mean the world to me. The honest to God truth is that no, I did not love or care about your mother, but that has nothing to do with you. You are my seed. You come from me. I would murder a nigga's ass dead over you."

"What about Jahliyah?"

"Her too. I don't see what you're seeing, but if it's because of somethin' that I said or did, I'm sorry." He took her hand and clasped his fingers into hers.

Natalia raised his hand and kissed the back of it. "Daddy, didn't you love Princess more than any other woman on earth?"

Taurus nodded. "Yeah, dat was my baby. There was nothing in this world that we wouldn't do for each other. We were at our lowest points together, and the highest." He lowered his head. "Damn."

"See, that's why I'm afraid. How long has it been since you've seen Jahliyah in the physical? I'm not talking about Facetiming or Zooming either."

Taurus switched over to the fast lane. "Not since she was six years old. Our family is crazy. They instilled some sick theories inside of Jahliyah's head."

"Like what?" Natalia looked over at him curiously.

Taurus continued to drive in silence. He flared his nostrils and sighed. "I don't know."

“Daddy, you said that you were going to be an open book. If that's true, then you have to tell me what they put inside of her head.”

“They had her grow up thinking that I was the one that killed her mother.”

There was a long silence in the car. The sounds of the tires rolling over the cracks in the highway seemed louder. Cars zipped by with their music playing loudly, trying their best to get a good look into who was driving the McLaren.

“Did you?” Natalia asked softly.

“Never. Princess was the love of my life. I would never harm her in any way, shape, form or fashion. As much as I hate to expose the real, yo’ grandmother wasn't wrapped too tight, and because of our off-limits relationship, she fell so deeply that she didn't want me to be with anybody else, and she killed both Princess and Blaze. It was the worst thing that ever happened to me. I'm still getting through it.”

Natalia shook her head and squeezed his fingers tighter. “Love is an amazing emotion that none of us will ever understand. You are an incredible man, Daddy, and maybe Grandma just felt like you were supposed to be hers and only hers. Lord knows that I've been there before.” She said this last part under her breath.

“What are you saying, that you've been there before? And remember that you are supposed to be an open book,” Taurus challenged her.

“Yeah.” Natalia sighed. “I really love Phoenix, and because of my love for him, I have gotten rid of three people - two at my own hands, and one by order. I don't want him loving anybody other than me and if he does, I will kill them just the same,” Natalia admitted. Her chest heaved up and down as she imagined the killings of the first Phoenix Junior, then of Alicia, and finally Bianca. She'd forgotten all about Kamaya, but she didn't feel like she'd gotten rid of her because of jealousy, whereas the others she could honestly admit that she had.

Taurus blew air out of his nostrils. “That's what I mean. The strength of our bloodline runs so deep that it has resided heavily within my own child. You most certainly get that all or nothing gene from your grandmother Deborah.”

“It’s good to know, because I was sure that I was just crazy for no reason.” She smiled weakly.

Taurus was silent for a long moment. “Baby, the first thing you have to realize is that our blood - your blood - is tainted. Some of the things that you feel aren't your fault, and there is no way to combat or resist them without feeling sick to your stomach. A person is only as strong as their DNA. So you can chop all of your weird feelings up to the things that I have placed inside of you through no fault of my own.”

Natalia smiled at him. “It's cool, Daddy. I love who I am, and how we are. I hate this world, and I don't want to be a part of it in a regular sense. Our family is everything to me, and I wouldn't change it or you for anything. We are who we are.” She kissed his cheek and allowed her lips to remain pressed there for a spell. When she took them away, she sat back in her seat and crossed her thighs. “Daddy?”

“Yeah, baby.”

“I don't wanna share you with Jahliyah. I want you all to myself. I've been thirsty for you ever since my mother explained to me who you were, and our family's history. While she thought she was making me want to never be around you, all she really did was make me crave and long for you in a way that I can't explain. Phoenix happened because it was the only way for me to feel that I was getting closer to you. Everything about mine and his relationship was nothing more than a placeholder for my Daddy Taurus. I'm just being honest.” She uncrossed her thighs and felt a trickle come from between her sex lips. She couldn't understand how the conversation that they were having was turning her on so much, but it was. Her clit poked out and rubbed against the satin material of her panties. She felt flushed.

Taurus laughed it off, oblivious to how serious Natalia really was. "Well, Precious, you ain't gotta worry about me loving nobody more than you. I love you and Jahliyah individually, and neither more than the other."

"Yeah, but here's the thing: that doesn't really work for me. You are my daddy, and just like I said, I want you all to myself. That's how I feel, and eventually that's what I am going to get whether you know it or not. But for now, it's cool. We'll play it your way. Now, I wanna know who you're trying to evade?"

"I kinda thought that would be your first question, but seeing that it wasn't, allow for me to explain things to you in a more physical sense." He looked over at her with a sly smile. "On some real shit though, baby, I'd be lying if I said that I didn't love the way you feel about me. It's been a while since anybody was as crazy as you are about me. That's why you're my baby."

Natalia shivered. "I'll kill somebody over you. I am literally crazy about you, and you're going to find that out real soon." She sat back in her seat and interlocked her fingers with his own. "I deserve all of you. That's how I feel."

With that said, she laid her head on his shoulder while her long hair blew out of the window and closed her eyes.

They rolled for the next twenty minutes in complete silence, heavy within their own minds.

Chapter 10

Jimmy Bands paced back and forth with anger surging through him worse than he could ever remember. He still couldn't believe how Gunnah had gotten down on him, and after all they'd been through together. He grew increasingly angry because of how many times he'd saved the man's life, both when they were teens and since they'd been young adults. He'd help to put food on Gunnah's mother's table when Gunnah was away doing a short bid upstate. Gunnah's mother Patty was an addict, addicted to The Rebirth that Taurus had made famous throughout the state of Tennessee. The Rebirth was a highly addictive heroin that took a hold of a user's mind, body, and soul. Once it had them, it both owned and conquered them in the most unimaginable ways. Jimmy Bands had taken pity on Patty and kept her supplied with The Rebirth while he paid all of her bills and kept food in her refrigerator. When she contracted the Coronavirus while Gunnah was upstate, it was Jimmy Bands that paid her hospital bills and made sure that she was nursed back to health with top of the line treatment. Gunnah knew about this, and yet he still chose to come at Jimmy Bands. This infuriated him.

"Say mane, I don't know why you steaming over dat fuck boy. You should have known that Blood was a hoe from the get go. Usually when you give a pussy any form of power, it tends to do too much," Rondo said before he lowered his head and tooted a thick line of pink coke. He fed both nostrils and coughed.

"Dese niggas ain't loyal, Blood. Fuck nigga gon' cap on me in front of everybody in the Mound. Make me look like a straight bitch. Nawl, potna, I ain't going for dat shit thurr. Plus the Mound gross every bit of two million dollars a week. Dat nigga Phoenix find out I lost the Mound to Gunnah and shit gon' hit the fan. I ain't trying to take that L. Fuck that."

Rondo laid his head back on the couch and cuffed his piece. "Mane, ya already know I'm ready to blow dat nigga's brains out of his head. You gimme the order, and that shit is as good as done. I'll stank his whole crib too: moms, daughter, son, baby mama…fuck 'em all! Dis that Duffle Bag shit here, my nigga, straight up. Orange Mound through and through."

Jimmy Bands kept pacing. He imagined Patty with two slugs in her face, and that made him feel a way. Even though she was an addict, she was still good people and he didn't want to see anything bad happen to her. He shook his head as a picture of Gunnah came across his mind's eye. He cringed and imagined how Gunnah would look laid out in a casket. That made him smile.

"Fuck you smiling at wit' yo' crazy ass?" Rondo sat forward and rested his elbows on his thighs.

Jimmy Bands balled his fingers into fists. "I was just thanking 'bout some shit, dat's all."

"Some shit like what?"

Before he could answer him, May Baby came to the den's door and knocked on it. "Jimmy, yo' sister just pulled up."

Jimmy Bands stopped mid-pace and rushed to the door. He pulled it open and shot past May Baby. By the time he got to the front door, Skyy was coming into the house with the key that Jimmy Bands had given her. He yanked the door open and snatched her into the house, picking her up along the wall.

"Bitch, if I find out that you fuckin' wit' the enemy, I'm finna murk yo' ass right here and right now." He tightened his hold on her Moschino top and forced her further into the wall.

Skyy was light caramel with brown eyes and shoulder-length permed hair that she kept whipped at one of the three salons that she owned. Her figure was slim, yet thick. She was small up top, and thick down low.

She smacked his hands. "Nigga, get yo ma'fuckin' hands off me, mane! I don't know what da fuck wrong wit-chu, but I ain't yo' chile!" she snapped, kicking her legs wildly.

Jimmy Bands held her up higher. Now her head was touching the ceiling. "Simple bitch, you fucking dat nigga Gunnah? Huh?"

Skyy tried to pry his hands from her clothes once again, to no avail. "Jimmy, let me down. You don't own me. You can't tell me what to do just 'cause you my big brother. Dis shit getting out of hand."

Jimmy slapped her and dropped her to the floor. "Dat mean you is."

Skyy crawled around on the floor, holding on to her face. Her eyes watered. She sat on her bottom and scooted backward until her back was against the wall. "Why I can't fuck wit' him, Jimmy? You never said that I couldn't. You told me to never fuck wit' a broke nigga that didn't have shit going for himself or couldn't afford me. In case you didn't know, Gunnah is getting money. That nigga pay all of my bills and my rental fees for my shops. He buys my supplies and pays my workers. Dat means I'm making a hundred percent profit. I ain't gotta pay nothin' but taxes. Dat seem like a bet to me."

"You sucking dat nigga dick too den? So dat's true too?" Jimmy imagined his sister going down on Gunnah and it made him want to throw up and commit mass murder at the same time."

"I'm eighteen, Jimmy. Why you worried 'bout how I get down behind closed doors? I don't worry 'bout what you do with May Baby, or whoever else. What you do is yo' bidness, and what I do is mine. Damn." She slowly made her way to her feet. "'Sides, long as he paying me, it shouldn't matter what I do, long as I'm coming out on top. Dat's what you taught me, and dat's what I live by."

Jimmy had begun to pace again. He stopped and looked back at her, almost ready to attack her. He hated himself for teaching her so many hood lessons. He wished that he could have instilled more values into her, but he didn't have them himself to instill. They were from the grimy slums of Memphis. You did what you had to, and you learned the lessons that allowed for you to survive the trenches. Their parents had allowed for them to be adults at a young age. They themselves were also consumed by the deadly trenches of Memphis.

"Who's putting my bidness in da streets? How do you know so much about my behind closed doors activities?" She walked up on him.

"Cuz that fuck nigga one-upped me today with that knowledge. Guess he tryna take over Orange Mound and saying dat all Duffle Bag Cartel members are outlawed from being in the hood. Niggas threatening death and all of dat garbage. But you should already know I ain't 'bout to accept dat shit laying down. You better get whatever you gon' get outta dat nigga, 'cause I'm 'bout to treat that trick. Straight up."

Skyy covered her mouth as she imagined all of her paid bills having to be handled by her. She didn't like what that looked like and immediately went into reconciliation mode. "Jimmy, you don't even care 'bout Orange Mound no more. You're rocking the fuck out of Harris County, and Clover Land got your name painted all over it. Why are you even tripping over Orange Mound? That turf is burned up anyway."

"Ain't 'bout da money, shawty. Don't no ma'fucka tell da Duffle Bag Cartel where dey can and can't go. That shit'll get a ma'fucka fucked over every time," Rondo slurred. He'd switched over to sipping syrup.

Skyy mugged him, disgusted. "Ain't nobody talking to yo' big ass. Dis is me and my brother speaking. Please mind yo' bidness, li'l one." She rolled her eyes.

"Only ma'fucka I let talk to me like dat is you, girl. Lucky you my nigga's sister. Dat's da truth right durr." He sipped from his syrup and laid back on the couch.

"Boy, bye. Ain't nobody thanking 'bout what you screaming. Anyway, Jimmy, why you can't let dis situation go?" She blocked his path and looked into his eyes.

"'Cause I'm about to be king of the Duffle Bag Cartel sooner than you thank, and ain't no ma'fucka finna make me look like a bitch da way dat nigga just did. So it's like I said. Hit dat nigga's pockets as much as you can over da next week, and den chop dat shit cause buddy as bout to rest in blood. Dat's on Mama. Now get da fuck outta my face. Every time I look at you now, I imagine you sucking dat nigga's dick." He flung her to the floor and stepped over her. "Let's roll, Slime."

Rondo got up on wobbly knees. He wiped his face with his hand. "Tick tock, li'l shawty. Tick muthafuckin' tock." He looked down at her as he and Jimmy Bands left the den.

Skyy covered her face with her hands after they left and cried her eyes out. She was so angry. She stood up and stomped her left foot. Tears rolled down her face. "Sometimes I hate you, Jimmy. I hate yo' fucking guts." She knocked over his flat screen television and left the den with the television smoking.

***

Phoenix opened the passenger's door to his cocaine white Beamer and allowed Jahliyah to sit inside of it. She smiled up at him and scooted away from the door, giving him the space to close it. Once it was closed, she leaned across the console to open his door for him. Phoenix got back inside of his car and slammed the door. Junior was in the back clicked into his booster seat. His eyes opened for a second and then closed again.

"I know yo' Pops gon' be happy as hell that you rolling into town early. He didn't thank you were gon' show up for a few weeks." Phoenix said this while pulling out of the airport parking lot.

"Well, I was gon' come when I told him I was, but I've been wanting to meet my old man my whole life. Now that I know he's out of that place and within reach, I just gotta see him before something crazy happens. Besides, I got some things that I have to place into his lap."

"Whew, shawty, you talk proper as hell. You must not be 'round nobody but white folk now or somethin'?" He laughed.

"Yeah, I'm a businesswoman now. When I left Memphis, I was just as country as the next bumpkin, but that speech doesn't get you nowhere in life that's worth going." She fastened her seatbelt and adjusted it so that it fit her frame. Jahliyah was 5'4" tall, caramel, with Asian-like features and natural wavy hair that stopped at the upper portion of her back. She was gorgeous and physically strapped like a top notch southern stripper. She was into fitness heavily, and even though she was, it did very little in the taking of her ass away. She was what men referred to as slim thick.

"I know I talk country as hell, but dat shit ain't stopping me from getting to da money. Shid, I wish a ma'fucka would knock me 'cause I got a southern twang. Dat'll be da day." His eyes trailed down to her thick thighs, which were barely covered by her Fendi pleated skirt. They were oiled, and the scent coming off of Jahliyah was Chanel and money. Phoenix knew without a shadow of a doubt that he was going to have to see what that pussy felt like. So far he'd fucked two of Taurus's daughters, and both had some of the best pussy he'd ever had in his life. Jahliyah, he hoped, would be his third.

"You in a whole other profession though, big cuz. Me, I'm in the cosmetics, real estate, and finance industry. I am forced to present myself in such a way. But trust me, dat hood shit still in there." She smiled, and dimples appeared on both cheeks. She reminded him of a prettier, younger version of Gabrielle Union-Wade.

Phoenix couldn't help checking her out, as much as he knew he shouldn't have been. His eyes trailed down to the swell of her caramel breasts. He stopped breathing for a split second and had to compose himself. "Yeah, well, I guess to each his own. You do what you gotta do to survive in this crazy world. Anyway, yo' Pops and Natalia gon' be gone until tomorrow morning. They taking care of some bidness. Dat means that you and I are going to get more acquainted."

Jahliyah raised her left eyebrow. "Oh, is that dat right? Aren't you the same individual that is supposed to be my cousin, and you got a baby by my sister?"

Phoenix started to cruise. "You already know how crazy our family is, so ain't no need for me to even answer dat question. Case you wondering, our son right back durr sleeping in dat car seat. Just as handsome as he wanna be. All ten fingers and toes."

Jahliyah glanced over her shoulder at the sleeping Junior. "What's dat supposed to mean?"

"Just saying, ain't shit wrong wit' my shawty, Dat's all. But I thank we getting too far ahead of da game. I'ma get a bit more acquainted wit' you, and we just gon' chill. After all, we family." He cheesed. He had in his five hundred thousand dollar diamond snatch out grill. It sparkled and glistened in the sunlight.

Jahliyah eyed it and shook her head. "Yeah, cuz one thing is for sure, I definitely ain't in New York anymore." She closed her eyes and thought about what it was going to be like to meet her father in person for the first time. She smiled and took a deep breath. "Is Taurus everythang that I'm thinking that he's going to be?"

Phoenix kept rolling. He looked over at her and shrugged his shoulders. "I don't really know what you're seeing. As far as I know, he's my uncle, he gets major money, and he's cool as a fan. Outside of that, I don't really know."

Jahliyah opened her left eye and looked over at him. "You tryna say that my daddy is still out here in these streets? At his age?"

Phoenix laughed. "The man is barely forty, and he look better den most of these young codeine pill heads running around. Far as him being in da streets...hell nawl. Once yo' paper reaches a certain status, you ain't gotta be in da streets no more. That's when you find true go-getters like me." Phoenix beamed with pride.

Jahliyah nodded. "Yeah, I guess I can see that dope boy stuff in you real tough. That's what's up. As long as it works for you. But anyway, I didn't sleep a wink on the plane. I was too busy worried about somebody coughing or sneezing on me. If it's all the same to you, I'ma get a bit of rest, and den I'ma be able to rub elbows with you. I don't mean to be rude." She yawned and covered her mouth.

"None taken. When we get to the South Beach gated community, I'ma wake you up. Until den, sleep easy." He smiled, and once again his eyes trailed down to her exposed thick thighs that were full of sheen. *Yeah, I gotta see what dis pussy like. Taurus's daughters be having dat bomb shit, and he loved Princess the most. Jahliyah is Princess's daughter, so her pussy gotta be fye*, he thought, switching lanes and increasing his speed in an attempt to get to their mansion as soon as he could. He wanted to spend some much-needed alone time with Jahliyah. He had more than a few tricks up his sleeve.

Chapter 11

Taurus waited patiently for Natalia to hop off of the private jet. She came down the steps that had been lowered for them and took a hold of his hand. Together they walked across the top of the U.S. Bank federal building. They were led into a door that was secured by six security guards that wore Coronavirus masks across their faces. As they stepped through the door they were patted down and breezed over with a metal detecting wand. Then both father and daughter were guided through a metal detector, and a wand was used once again. From there, they were led down a long carpeted hallway that curved into a hallway with white linoleum floors. That hallway stopped and connected with a boardroom. At the door of the boardroom were two Secret Service men. Once again, both Taurus and Natalia were patted down, and a metal detecting wand was used on them. After they were cleared, Taurus was allowed to pass first, and then Natalia.

Inside, the boardroom had a long wood grain table with twenty-two chairs. There were twenty along the sides, and one chair at each end. At the far end of the table with two Secret Servicemen standing behind him was Don Jr. He had a head full of brown hair plugs with a slight coat of makeup on his aging face. He sat with his fingers clasped and a look of superior dominance written across his face. He eyed Taurus, and then Natalia.

"Usually before you meet someone of my importance, you announce that you are bringing a guest, especially when it is one as controversial as this one who stands beside you.

Natalia lowered her eyes at Don Jr. "Daddy, what on earth would you have to do with this corrupt Trump family? I can only imagine." She said this distastefully.

Don Jr. laughed and ordered both Taurus and Natalia to sit. After they followed his commands, he continued. “The last person that should be calling anybody corrupt, Natalia, is you. You are wanted by your own Russian family for the murder and robbery of your own mother and grandfather. You betrayed your people and crossed over to your African American side of the family only after you bled your Russian side dry. You've had an agenda from the day Nastia gave birth to you, and it’s sad to see that your agenda manifested itself into her untimely execution. Why, do you know what the great Putin would render to myself and my father if I were to turn you over to him this moment?”

Though all of this information was somewhat of a blindside to Taurus, he stood up. “Ain't nobody gon' lay a finger on my daughter. Shit happens. We move on with our lives, and that's that. As of this moment, she resides under me.”

Don Jr. looked up at Taurus, unimpressed. “You assassinate key leaders in Congress and already you feel entitled?” Don Jr. laughed. “You owe us far more than that, so let's stop it with the demands on her behalf.”

“Your family isn't even as connected as you make it seem. Donald is more than five hundred million dollars in debt to my loyal family side of the Kremlin. If you even think about touching one sandy brown hair on my head, the Trump name will be remembered for nothing more than tragedy and assassinations in the world’s most grotesque way. And when I say this, I mean they will be on the receiving end. Now test me, bitch!” Natalia slammed her hand on the table and peered her blue eyes into the hazel ones of Don Jr., spooking him. He broke eye contact, and Natalia scooted closer to Taurus.

Taurus broke the silence. “I am here. Why did your father call this meeting?”

Don Jr. waved out the Secret Servicemen. They were reluctant to leave, especially after the things that Natalia had said, but one by one they filed out, leaving Don Jr. alone and vulnerable. He took a deep breath and leaned forward in the big leather chair. "The virus. We need for more of your people to catch it. The last consensus that was taken shows that white America is vastly becoming the majority, as we stated to you before. The only way to combat this is to infect as many of your people as possible and then get them to take the vaccine that will be injected into them. That will cause them to become sterile, or weak seed bearers. Our goal, as you know, will be to, in twenty years' time, reign as the most dominant and most superior race on earth. To be able to make this come into fruition, we must weaken, sicken, and annihilate as many of your people as possible, and it starts with the ruse of the Coronavirus." He sat back and kicked his feet up on the desk.

"Daddy, what is he talking about? Why am I getting the impression that you are working with these white supremacists of the government to hurt and ultimately erase our people?" Natalia was in shock.

Don Jr. covered his mouth. "Oops, did I say too much while the baby was in the room?" He laughed, and immediately his expression changed to that of hatred.

Taurus took a deep breath and exhaled. "I can explain all of this later, Natalia. Right now, I need to find out what my tasks are so that I can enter into the next phases of our lives."

"The next phase? The next fuckin' phase? This sicko is telling you to commit genocide on our people, and you sit here as if he's not speaking like he's lost his freaking mind." She bucked her eyes and stood up. "I can't be here right now. I-I gotta go." She yanked her hand away from Taurus. She glared over at Don Jr. "You and your father just don't know how to accept defeat. You should be ashamed of yourself in every way. And Daddy, you disappointed me." She turned and left the board room.

Taurus lowered his head to his lap. "Give me the things that I need. The biochemicals and all. I will make it happen. You have my word."

Don Jr. sat back and sparked a cigar. "You damn right you will, Taurus. You will, because you owe the government. You're a free man, all because of us. You're under our protection, but as soon as you choose to step outside the chains of your slavery..." He ran a finger across his heck. "Dead; just another dead nigger. We'll be in touch. You're dismissed."

***

Taurus stepped out of the shower that night, got dressed with the exception of his shirt, and stepped out of the hotel's bathroom. He saw that Natalia stood on the balcony of the Presidential suite smoking a stuffed blunt of Kush. When he stepped into the doorway, she looked over her shoulder at him, rolled her eyes, and proceeded right back to smoking. Taurus came further on to the balcony and slipped his arms around her waist, pulling her to him. She tensed and tried to pry herself loose at first, but after he nuzzled his face into the crux of her neck, she submitted to being held by him.

"I'm so disappointed in you, Daddy. I would have never imagined such a thing. You're no better than the Trump family."

Taurus kissed her neck and bit into it. "Shhh, baby, you only think like that because you don't truly know your father."

Natalia dropped the blunt over the edge of the balcony. She leaned back into him and wiggled her voluptuous bottom into his lap. She felt him harden and groan into her neck. "Daddy, what are you doing?"

Taurus rubbed his hands up her ribs and over her breasts. He cuffed them and slid them on down her hips. He pulled her back into him again. "I don't know what it is about you, Natalia, but you make me feel shit I shouldn't be feeling. Whenever you're in my presence, I feel this crazy urging that drives me insane." He slipped her tight white beater upward until her skin was exposed. He rubbed her stomach and further upward until he was cuffing her breasts again. Her nipples were rock hard and throbbing.

Natalia panted and swallowed what looked spit her mouth could conjure. "Daddy, you know I can't control the way you're making me feel. If we don't stop right now, we're going to cross a line that we can never step back over." She turned around to face him, looking directly into his eyes. Her arms went around his neck, as they usually did. "Did you hear what I said, Daddy?"

Taurus slid his hands around and cuffed her ass. He rolled the flesh, and then nearly picked her up by the cheeks. He kissed her neck and sucked on it. "Daddy wants you so bad, baby. I've been wanting you ever since I laid eyes on you. I don't care who you are to me." He rubbed under her ass cheeks until he was rubbing her hot pussy mound through her thong panties. His fingers managed to locate a hint of a sex lip that had slipped out of the material.

As soon as Natalia felt his finger touch her skin, she shivered and spaced her feet. "Daddy, I need you too. I don't care about nothing. Fuck the world. You're my daddy. Please take me. I been waiting for this my whole life."

Taurus picked her up and carried her into the hotel room. He kicked the door closed and fell on the bed with her, between her thick thighs. Natalia wrapped them around him and moaned into the crux of his neck. She bit him and dug her nails into his back. Taurus shivered. Natalia sat up slightly to suck on his earlobe. Her tongue dared to venture inside of it. Taurus groaned and trembled.

"Wait a minute, baby, we can't. This ain't right. You're my baby girl, and I love you more than to get down like this with you." He started to back up.

Natalia kept her thighs tightened around his waist. She sat all the way with her hands wrapped around his neck and looked into his eyes. "Daddy, please. My whole life all I've ever wanted was to be loved by you in this way. It's dominated my every fantasy and every dream. Please don't deny me this." She kissed his lips and sucked on each one individually.

Taurus returned her kisses for a full minute until he was breathing heavy, and hard as a rock. He laid her back, grinding into her middle. Natalia opened her thighs wide and humped into him to feel him better. She was so wet that it oozed to her ass cheeks.

"Daddy, take me right now. Please; I need you." She laid back to show her submission.

Taurus trailed his tongue along her neck and stopped after feeling her reach between them and squeeze his hard piece. It throbbed in her hand. He backed up. "Nawl, baby, I can't do this. I would never forgive myself."

He started to get off of the bed once again after untangling her thighs from around his waist. He was wishing that he hadn't gone nearly a year without sex because now his body was craving the wrong things he felt, and his rotten DNA was getting the better of him. He was a foot from backing off of the bed when Natalia grabbed a hold of him again.

"Daddy, wait. I wanna show you something."

Chapter 12

Taurus sat on the edge of the bed, attentive, as Natalia stepped before him. She stood between his open muscular thighs. She stepped closer until her stomach was directly in his face.

"Daddy, you weren't there for me when I got these." She lifted her shirt just enough to show Taurus her stomach. Her fingers played over the sparse stretch marks there. "I needed you, and you weren't there for me, and it's because of these that I feel so ugly."

Taurus took his fingers and rubbed over each mark one at a time as if experiencing a new feat that he found fascinating. "Baby, there is nothing wrong with you. You are perfect in every single way. Look at you."

"But that's not how I feel. I don't feel perfect. I feel ugly." Her eyes watered.

Taurus saw her on the verge of tears and turned his attention back to her stomach. "I'm sorry for not being there, li'l baby. My life has been so complicated. Ever since these people helped me to avoid the death penalty, they've had me by the balls. I couldn't risk the health and safety of you or Junior. Y'all are always my first priorities." He continued to rub her stomach.

"Even though you weren't there, even though you weren't in my life at the time, I still named my son after you. He still shares your name and your lineage. I've always been crazy about my Daddy." She took the back of Taurus's head and led him to her stomach.

Taurus kissed her stomach softly at first. He rubbed his face all over it, and then licked the length of each mark before nipping at her soft flesh with his teeth. "You're perfect, baby. I'd kill a nigga over you quicker than a heartbeat." He kissed some more and pulled her closer by her ass.

Natalia moaned. "Phoenix looks at me differently because of these stretch marks, Daddy. I can tell. He hasn't said anything, but I can tell."

Now Taurus was sucking all over her stomach. He kissed and rubbed his face all over it again. "Fuck Phoenix. You don't need no nigga to appreciate you. That's what Daddy here for."

Natalia moaned again and pulled her shirt over her head. She tossed it to the floor and stood there nude from the waist up. Taurus didn't hesitate to take a hold of her breasts. He squeezed them before picking her up and tossing her back on the bed. He lowered his head and took his time sucking her long nipples. His tongue trailed circles around them one at a time, then he was pulling with his lips.

Natalia arched her back. She slipped her hand between her thighs and into her panties. She was soaking wet. Her middle finger played over her erect clit so that greasy trails of secretions stuck to it. "Mmm, Daddy. Touch me. I don't care. Just do it."

Taurus ripped her panties down her thighs and off. He dropped them beside her on the bed and slowly opened her thighs wide. Before him, her shaved pussy looked extra meat and glossy. Her juices flowed heavily. Her clit stood at the top of her lips like a pinky finger. He could smell her scent and it drove him crazy. He leaned forward and kissed her pussy. "You sho' you wanna do this, li'l baby?"

In response, Natalia stuck her hand between her thighs and opened her pussy lips wide for him. Her pink was on full display. "Do me, Daddy. I need you. I need you so bad."

Taurus hesitated for a moment. He closed his eyes and took a deep breath, trying to find the will to walk away, to leave the bedroom so that he could clear his mind, because he knew once they crossed that bridge, that there was no turning back. "Baby, I—"

Natalia sensed his reluctance. She reached out for him and stuffed his face between her thighs. Taurus went crazy. He opened her wide and performed tricks on her clitoris that drove her insane. In a matter of seconds, she was humping into his face and screaming for him. His tongue dug deep and stabbed her box at full speed before he pulled it out and sucked hard on her pearl's tongue. Natalia forced his face further into her gap again. She screamed and came in jets, coating his bottom lip and then the sides of his neck.

"Daddy! Daddy! Oh shit, Daddy! I love you so much. I love you so much," she whimpered.

Taurus flipped her over and kissed all over her ass cheeks. He sucked them one at a time and separated the mounds. Her crinkle revealed itself. He took his tongue and made love to her back door. He slipped a finger deep into her bowels before he pulled it out and sucked all over her again back there. He made her rise to her knees and spread them. Once in this position he proceeded to eat her from the back while his nose remained in her asshole.

Natalia fell to her chest whimpering and moaning. She closed her eyes and couldn't believe that Taurus was finally touching her. The man that she'd craved for her entire life was finally sending her into a whirlwind of sexual delight. "Unnnn! Unnnn! Daddy, oooh, shit, Daddy! I love you so much." She threw her head back and came hard.

Taurus backed up off of the bed. They'd gone too far. He knew it. He had to stop. He couldn't exceed this level, as much as he wanted to. "Okay, baby. Damn, I fucked up. Let's go to sleep now. Gon' clean yourself up."

Natalia turned around with both Russian and Stevens' bloodline of passion running through her. "Sleep? Are you kidding me?" She yanked down his pants, along with his boxers. She took a hold of his huge dick and pumped it up and down.

Seconds later, her mouth was fitted over the round head and she was sucking like her mouth depended on it while Taurus squeezed her booty, and fingered her pussy from the back at full speed. He pulled his fingers out every so often and sucked them into his mouth. Natalia sucked harder. She would pop him out and rub his dick all over her face.

"I'm a Daddy's girl. I'm my Daddy's girl. Fuck, I love my Daddy." She sucked him back in and deep throated him as best she could.

Taurus groaned. His knees threatened to buckle. He moaned out loud. He took hold of her long hair and forced her to gag on his pipe. "I'm finna cum, baby. Fuck, Daddy finna cum. Where you want it? Where you want it, baby?"

Natalia took a hold of his thighs and forced him deeper into her throat just as he came in thick ropes. The first feel of it caused her to cum harder than she could ever remember. Taurus shook and kept fingering her harder and harder while her pussy sucked at his digits. He pulled out of her mouth and came all over her pretty face. Skeet after skeet. She took a hold of his dick again and pumped it more and more until it only leaked his seed. Then she licked the length of him and sucked him until she had cleaned him all the way up. They collapsed on the bed with her pumping his dick.

"Daddy, I wanna fuck now. Please. I want you to put this inside of me. I need it." She opened her thighs and showed him her pussy again.

Taurus rubbed her lips and slipped his fingers inside of her. He sank them deep. "Boo, I wanna hit this pussy too, but I feel like we've done enough for one night. Let's sleep on it, and if we still like we wanna proceed forward in the morning, then we'll spend another day together. But if remorse sets in, then this will be just between us, and we'll forgive each other. You understand me?"

Natalia shook her head. "I'm not gon' feel a way. I don't think that we did anything wrong. We love each other, and we belong to each other. Screw this world. I want my daddy." She rolled over and wound up on top of him. She leaned her face down and kissed his lips. "Daddy, why do I feel like I feel? Why have I been craving you ever since I came into this world? Is there somethin' wrong with me?"

Taurus ran his hands down and all over her ass cheeks. He squeezed them. "Nawl, baby. I gave you that blood. It ain't yo' fault, just like dis right here ain't yo' fault. I should have been strong enough to resist you. I'm the one that's fucked up in the head."

Natalia shook her head. "I'm glad that you didn't. Had you done that, Daddy, my self-esteem really would have fallen. The fact that you don't want to lay me all the way down is enough to drive me crazy already. I deserve you. I deserve you more than anybody else walking this earth, including Jahliyah." She frowned.

Taurus pulled her down so that her head was resting on his chest. His big hands ran up and down her back. "Baby, you ain't gotta worry about me loving nobody more than I love you. You are my world, and even though we are still figuring each other out, I already know that I will not be closer to anybody than I am with you."

Natalia climbed up his body and kissed his lips. She ran her hands all over his muscular chest and shoulders. Her finger slid down the crease of his eight pack, all the way down until she was cuffing his dick. It grew in her hands. "What if I still wanna fuck you in the morning, Daddy? I mean, I already know that I am, but what if I want you really, really bad tomorrow Will you lay me down? Please?" She licked his nipple and pumped his piece.

Taurus couldn't stop himself from getting harder and harder. "We just gotta see, boo. I wanna show you a few more things that I am into out in that world, and then we'll go from there. But you gotta know that I want you just as bad as you want me, if not more."

Natalia rubbed her pussy all over his pipe and bent the head downward, sucking an inch of it into her hole, before Taurus pulled her off of it. She groaned. "Fuck, I just want my daddy right now. I don't wanna think about tomorrow. Please, Daddy, at least finger this pussy so I can take the edge off. Something. I'm burning up down there." She opened her thighs and sank down on his dick again, this time taking two inches of him. Her eyes rolled into the back of her head. She licked all over her lips, and once again, Taurus pulled her off of his pipe. "Damn Daddy."

Taurus laid her on her side and slid behind her. He bit into the back of her neck and held her tightly. "Fight the urge, baby. Tomorrow is another day. I love you. Now fall back."

Natalia shivered for an hour straight while Taurus held her. Finally, her eyes became heavy. Taurus kissed her cheek over and over and rubbed her hair for her. He kept her in a tight embrace, and after much resistance, she finally drifted off to sleep, feeling more crazy about him than she had about anybody in her entire life.

Chapter 13

Jimmy Bands stepped into the trap warehouse and wiped sweat from his brow. There was so much coke smoke in the air that it made it hard for him to breathe. On top of that, Houston was experiencing one of the hottest days of the year. It was a hundred and ten degrees outside, and the humidity made it feel like it was every bit of a hundred and thirty. He stopped after a couple paces inside of the warehouse and took a deep breath. Cursed with asthma and bronchitis whenever the weather was as bad as it was it often made it hard for him to breathe. He took his pump out of his pocket and took a few hits of it. It took a second, and then he felt better. He pulled his red bandana over his nose and proceeded forward with his ten man security team behind him.

The warehouse had at one point in time been a slaughter house. But after a bunch of renovations, Phoenix had dropped the cash to turn it into his cook, smoke, sorting, and packaging post. He had his trusted dope boys come from all over Houston to sit in the trap warehouse three times a week to break down a ton of coke, boy, and meth. Once the products were broken down, they were packaged and loaded into semi-trucks and vans and then they were distributed all over Texas, Arizona, and Tennessee. Phoenix's goal was to invade other states, but that was extremely tricky because each state belonged to a certain cartel. And often those cartels were controlled by bosses that had pulled over the President of the United States, so to cross them or to invade their turf was to start a war that couldn't end in anything other than mass bloodshed. Oftentimes the federal government looked the other way, and that opened up a can of worms.

Phoenix, at the moment, was content with the three states that he had, and just like every other cartel that had a strong lethal boss behind them, he did as well. Atop the throne of the Duffle Bag Cartel he officially sat, but even higher than him was Taurus. Taurus was plugged all over the world. He had mob ties to bosses that didn't even speak English. Taurus represented a boss that only few would ever be able to set eyes on while they were in the game. Though he put up a front as a regular man, Taurus was levels ahead of the game. Phoenix didn't fully understand how he'd risen to his place, but he respected it, and he stayed in his lane.

Jimmy Bands, under Phoenix, was given full control over the trap warehouse. It was his job to make sure that everything ran smoothly and that Phoenix received his proper cash at the end of each week. Phoenix controlled the drug trade and Jimmy Bands controlled the flow. Because of their understanding, the Duffle Bag Cartel and its members were eating like never before. Even the poorest member of their crew was seeing no less than a hundred thousand dollars. While to most that may have not been a lot of money, in reality, most of the niggas in the hood trapping would never even get a chance to see fifty G's. That was a fact, so Jimmy felt that all was well.

Jimmy Bands walked around the warehouse making sure that everything was flowing like a well-oiled machine. There were twenty tables breaking down kilos of The Rebirth. Twenty masked people were on each side of the table. On one side they would be breaking down the bricks and separating them into the appropriate amount for packaging. After that amount was weighed and confirmed, they slid it across the table to their teammate, who aluminum foiled it up and dropped it into a Cartel-stamped Ziploc. Once the Ziploc was filled to capacity, they dropped it into a duffle bag. Once the duffle bag was full, it was zipped and stacked inside of a semi-truck. This went on and on until the entire shipment was crushed, weighed, bagged, and tagged for distribution.

When it came to the coke, Phoenix made sure that Jimmy Bands and the Duffle Bag Cartel imported only the best from the coke fields of Columbia. Straight fish scale, pink, and potent, with a ninety-five percent or higher purity rating. Jimmy Bands was responsible for making sure that his workers separated the coke and shipped it to the record studios, strip clubs, and suburbs, while other facets of the coke were cooked and turned into rock and poured into the ghettos of Texas, Tennessee, and Arizona. Oftentimes the coke would be hit with meth to strengthen its longevity for the user. This was a delicate process that Taurus had given Phoenix the recipe for, and Phoenix had passed it along to Jimmy Bands and Jimmy Bands' chosen workers that dealt specifically with coke and meth. After assuring that everything was flowing properly with the coke, Jimmy turned his attention to the meth part of the operations.

Jimmy Bands didn't let nobody touch his meth other than the twenty-five Asians that he had in charge of it. These Asians worked miracles with the crystal. They had a way of making it look like pure glass, and the potency was so good that it kept the addicts looking solely for the Duffle Bag Cartel stamp. This was important because the Duffle Bag Cartel was at war in sales with so many cartels out of Mexico that often the game seemed cluttered. When it became too cluttered, a war was necessary to clear the path for money. The only thing about that was when a war was in motion, the money slowed, and a narcotics organization like the Duffle Bag Cartel lost millions until the war was finalized while other Cartels raked in those millions. War was ugly, and only necessary to clear the path for mass cash and influence.

By the time Jimmy Bands walked out of the warehouse and jumped into his cherry red Ferrari, he felt confident that everything was flowing the way that it was supposed to.

It was 9:30 later that night when he pulled up on May Baby. She slowly came down the steps with her cell phone to her ear, talking a mile a minute to one of her bottle girls at one of her three strip clubs. The girl was irritated over the fact that she'd been promised to start in the VIP section and she had not been placed there when her shift started that night. May Baby had forgotten and scheduled another female to be there. She assured her that she would start at the end of the week, and that since she was patient, she would book her for two additional weeks. After reconciling this problem, she ended the call, just as Jimmy Bands stepped out of his Ferrari fitted in Louis Vuitton from head to toe. His neck was flooded with ice, and his piece had a Duffle Bag Cartel emblem on it with crushed green diamonds. It had been a present from Phoenix for Jimmy's eighteenth birthday.

May Baby came down the steps and slipped into his arms. Her Gucci skirt dress clung to her body like a second skin. She fell into Jimmy Bands' arms and closed her eyes, feeling him wrap his biceps around her.

"Damn, baby, today has been so strenuous. I don't know why I ain't let you stop me when I got to the second strip club. Trying to run three is driving me crazy, and that's with two degrees in business."

Jimmy Bands laughed and kissed the side of her forehead. "Dat's dat grind right thurr, shawty. Ain't finna feel sorry fo' yo' ass. Everybody gotta be able to contribute to the bigger goal at hand. Even my bitch knows how many days I be tired and feeling like I'm tired of trapping."

May Baby rolled her eyes. "Damn, baby, sometimes you can just be a little compassionate and let me have it. I know dis shit ain't easy, but just hearing that you understand would be enough for me." She finished her hug and headed to the Ferrari.

Jimmy Bands cursed under his breath. “Damn, shawty, Dat’s my fault. You got dat. Hurr.” He slipped a jewelry box from his inside coat pocket and handed it to her. “Dis just to let you know dat I'm fuckin' wit’ you the long way.”

May Baby opened the box and pulled out the pink iced Patek. Her eyes got big. “Dis the female Patek that just dropped? Really, baby?” She dropped the box, slipped her wrist into the band, and then clasped it around her. Even though it was nighttime, the street light caused the diamonds to twinkle brightly. She ran up and hugged him. “Thank you, baby.”

Jimmy Bands cuffed her ass and held her. “It’s good, shawty. You deserve at least dat. Now come on. We ’bout to head to Dallas so we can kick back at the Supreme.”

May Baby kissed his cheek and smiled. “Dat’s why I'm so crazy ’bout yo’ ass. It's cuz you always doing shit like dis. Ride or die for you, Jimmy, that's on everythang. It's ride or die for my nigga.”

Jimmy Bands walked around to the other side of the Ferrari. He laughed. “Yeah, shawty, I guess we gon' see ’bout dat.”

***

Gunnah took his razor blade and chopped through the heroin that sat on the table in front of him. He pulled his nose and ran a handkerchief in and out of it to make sure that it was dry. He separated his dope into eight thin lines and took one up each nostril hard. After vacuuming it up, he tilted his head backward and pinched his nostrils closed. The drug took seconds to course all over him. He shut his eyes and began to shake. He swallowed his spit and smiled weakly.

Skyy sat across the table from him. “I still don't understand why you gotta do this shit. You out here catching all of dis money. You got all of dese dumb-ass niggas following you, and instead of you doing right, you're sitting here shoveling dis shit up yo' nose. Man, dis is da stupidest shit I done ever seen in my life." She took a sip from her bottled water.

Gunnah opened his eyes and mugged her. He was so high that he was seeing two of her. "Shut up, bitch." He wiped his nose and closed his eyes again briefly.

"Excuse me?"

"You heard what the fuck I said. Every time you come around me while I'm doing my thang, you gotta cap off at the gums. Every ma'fucka in the hood got a vice. I like to treat my nose a li'l bit. Fuck so wrong wit' dat? It ain't stopping everybody from eating."

Skyy looked him over for a moment. She shook her head. "What I tell you 'bout calling me out of my name like you be doing the rest of those hoes in Orange Mound? Dis ain't dat. You gon' give me my fuckin' respect, because I don't carry it like those other ratchet-ass bitches."

Gunnah sat up and curled his upper lip. "Shawty, on da Mound, if you don't shut the fuck up, I'm 'bout to punish go yappity yap ass. Now shut the fuck up!" he snapped.

"I don't know who you thank you be talking to, but you don't strike no fear in my heart. You ain't gon' treat me like some bimbo either. I don't give a fuck who you thank you is." She shook her head. "You know what? I'm outta here." She stood up from the table inside of Gunnah's living room, ready to leave.

Gunnah eyed the back of her head. "Shawty, sit yo' ass down fo' I get up."

Skyy placed her purse over her shoulder by the strap. "Gunnah, I don't care 'bout you getting up. You don't spook me. I'm leaving. I don't like when you are geeked up on dat shit. So

I'ma holler at you when you come down. Later, nigga." She walked out of the room.

Gunnah jolted out of the chair and closed the distance between them in four strides. He grabbed Skyy by the back of the neck and slammed her face first into the wall. She groaned in pain. He turned her around and backhanded her so hard that she twisted and fell to the ground, bleeding from the mouth, both dazed and lost.

"I told you 'bout playing wit' me, didn't I. Didn't I tell you 'bout fuckin' wit a boss?"

Skyy covered her mouth. She could feel the blood pouring through her fingers. She slowly tried to climb to her feet. "Awright, Gunnah, I fucked up. I'm sorry. I can see that I'm getting on yo' nerves, so I'm just gon' bounce and get up with you at another time." Skyy knew that when Gunnah was high that he was crazy and extremely abusive. She didn't want any parts of him while he was under the influence of heroin. She rose and slowly began to back away from him, bleeding from the lips.

"I pay all of yo' bills, don't Im bitch? I make sure that you got everythang that you need, and you still like capping off. What the fuck am I supposed to do, huh? How do I handle a hard headed bitch like you?"

Skyy backed up a few more feet. She swallowed her spit. Suddenly her lip began to swell and pound in pain. "I'm sorry, Gunnah. I swear to God, I'm sorry. Please just give me a pass. I won't mess up no more."

Gunnah saw how her lips were swelling up, and his eyes grew big. He furrowed his brows and became even angrier than before. "All you finna do is go tell yo' bitch-ass brother, ain't you? Dat's the only thang you finna do."

Skyy backed up some more and held her arms at full length. "No, I'm not. I don't tell my brother everything. What me and you got going on ain't got nothing to do with him," she swore.

Gunnah shook his head. "Nawl, bitch, I know yo' type. You finna go holler at dat nigga and den da next thang I know, we gon' be trying to fan each other down over a bitch. Fuck I look like?" He grabbed her by the throat and slammed her into the wall so hard that she left an imprint in the drywall.

Skyy yelped and closed her eyes. The back of her head was screaming like a white chick in a scary movie. "Please, Gunnah. I swear I ain't gon' tell him shit. I wouldn't betray you like that. Plus I brought dis shit on myself. Next time I know to do better. I'm sorry, baby." Skyy wanted to do anything to deter Gunnah from hurting her further. She was more than aware of his quick temper, and she knew that he could, in fact, kill her, have his men dispose of her body, and nobody would ever hear from her again. Those facts were enough to drive her over the edge.

Gunnah pulled his .45 from the small of his waistband and pressed the barrel to her forehead. He lowered his eyes. "Say, shawty, long as I'm putting money in yo; purse and paying yo; bills, I'll beat the fuck out of you as much as I want to. You run under me. That means dat you my ma'fuckin' property. Next time you gon' keep yo mouth closed, and shut da fuck up when I say dat shit thurr. You feeling me on dat?"

"Yes, baby, I am." She shivered.

Gunnah loved the power and control he had over such a beautiful woman. It was enough to make him feel like he ran the entire world instead of just Orange Mound. He ran the gun along the side of her cheek. "You love me, shawty?"

Not only did Skyy not love him; she hated his guts. She felt that he was nothing more than a dope fiend, a bully, who'd gotten lucky enough to fall into the leadership position over the dope boys and trap stars of Orange Mound. “Yeah, baby, I love you. You're the only man that I have ever loved. I'm crazy about you,” she lied. *Nawl, nigga, I really don't, but I love having my bills paid. As soon as I figure out the codes to your safes, you're a dead man. That's on my mama*, she thought as he stroked her cheek.

“Yeah, bitch, I know you do. How couldn't you? I'm the reason you're able to do the shit that you do.” He laughed. “Get down on yo’ knees and bow to me.”

Skyy didn't hesitate. She knelt on both knees and lowered her head to the ground. “I'm sorry, baby. I surrender to you.” *You're going to be the first nigga I enjoy killing. I ain't never did it before, but Lord knows you got it coming.*

Gunnah unzipped his pants and stroked his piece after pulling it out. She placed the small head on her lips. “Take care of dis until I splash in yo’ shit. Yeah, bitch, handle all of dis meat.”

All what meat? Skyy laughed in her mind. She took a hold of his four inch wee-wee with her fingers and took a deep breath before sucking him into her mouth. If sucking his thing was the only way she was going to be able to walk out of there alive, then she'd have to do what she had too. She'd be forced to disregard the pain from her lips. She slurped his noodle until he was moaning at the top of his lungs. Literally thirty seconds later he was cumming and falling to his knees, whimpering like a punk. Skyy was disgusted, but intent on playing her role until she got the codes.

Chapter 14

I can't believe his punk ass gon' force me to walk all the way to the other side of town. He took my money, my purse, and my phone - for what? To teach me a lesson. Ugh, I hate niggas. After Gunnah's punk ass, I'm done with all black or hood niggas. I'ma find me a white boy, Skyy thought as she walked the dark streets of Memphis, headed to the north side of town, where Jimmy Bands had her put up in a lavish hotel. She was twenty blocks away from Orange Mound, and already her feet were killing her. It probably didn't help that she was rocking Dooney and Burke wedges and they were causing great pain on her arches.

She continued to stroll. More than one car had already stopped to blow their horn at her. Two of them thought that she was on the hoe stroll, and another was simply enamored of her rounded ass that was sitting up right in her Gucci jeans. She cursed out loud. "Man, I hope my brother lets me torture his bitch ass when he's ready to finish him."

She waited until the lights gave her the right of way before she crossed Martin Luther King Drive's busy intersection. She was in the middle of the street when Rondo pulled up in his Benz truck and blew his horn. Already irritated by the constant horn blowing from other people, she ignored him, and didn't even think to see who was blowing the horn at her.

Rondo slowed at the side of her and rolled down his passenger's window. He had a redbone sitting in the passenger's seat of his whip that he'd just picked up from the strip club. He'd had plans on flipping her in every way imaginable and she was down for the cause.

"Say, Skyy, fuck you doing out here dis late at night, shawty?"

Skyy froze and turned toward the familiar voice. When she saw that it was Rondo's truck, she felt a sigh of relief. “Damn, boy, you scared the shit out of me. What are you doing on dis side of town?”

Rondo pulled along the curb and got out. When he made it around to her, he took a hold of her arm and pulled her away from the passenger's side of his whip. He even rolled the window up with his remote. “Say, mane, dat bitch nigga Gunnah got you out here selling pussy, shawty? If he do, I'm finna smoke dat nigga tonight. Fuck what Jimmy talking ’bout.” He tightened his grip on her arm.

Skyy yanked her arms away from him. “Nawl, boy, ugh! Fuck I look like selling pussy for any nigga? If I was gon' do some shit like dat, I'd work for myself.”

“What, shawty? Mane shut dat shit up fo’ I pop you in yo’ ma’fuckin’ mouth. We have way too much money to ever have you stoop so low. You see how I'm riding, and your brother holding more den me.” He mugged the strip they were standing in, looking for potential jackers. “Fuck you doing out here dis late walking? And who did dis shit to yo’ mouth?” He grabbed her by the jaw and held her roughly.

“Stop, Rondo, damn.” She smacked his hand away. “Just let me get in and I'll explain everythang den.”

Rondo took a hold of her arm. He chirped his alarm and opened the passenger's door. The redbone inside was nodding her head to the music coming out of his speakers. “Say, bitch, get the fuck out my shit. Shawty finna take dat seat.”

“Damn, it's two in the morning! How the fuck I'm s’posed to get home?” she whined, looking at him and hoping to find an ounce of humanity.

“I don't know, and I don't give a fuck. Get up out my shit so shawty can sit thurr. Hurry up fo’ I throw you out,” he warned.

She stared at him for a second to make sure that he was serious, and then she cursed and grabbed her knock-off Birkin bag from between her legs. “You bogus for dis. Damn, you could have left me at the club den.”

“Hurry yo’ ass up.” Rondo grabbed her arm and pulled her out. She fell to the ground. Skyy felt sorry for her, but she already knew how the Duffle Bag Cartel got down. They were untamed savages, and there was nothing that anybody could do about it.

The redbone backed onto the sidewalk. “You bet’ not never come back to the club. I'ma make sure all the dancers know that you bad bidness.” She got on her phone and was ready to call a ride when a car looking for a street walker slowed and beeped at her. She waved the white man down, jogged up to his car, and got inside. It pulled off, but not before she could flip Rondo the bird by use of her middle finger.

Rondo was too busy helping Skyy into his truck to notice. He closed the door once she was all the way in. He jogged around and was about to get back into the truck when two masked men ran out of the alley toward his Benz with the intentions of laying him down.

Rondo rushed to the driver's side. “Shawty, get down, now!” Skyy followed his orders. Rondo grabbed a Draco from his back seat and turned around with it already cocked and loaded with a hundred shots. “Fuck niggas! Dis ain't dat. Duffle Bag, bitch!”

Boom! Boom! Boom! Boom!

The jackers took off running in separate directions. In a haste to make a clean getaway, one of them fell and twisted his ankle. He tried to jump up, but Rondo was on him immediately. Rondo stood over him and aimed.

Boom! Boom! Boom! Boom!

The jacker shook uncontrollably before his life left his body. Rondo took off behind the other one. He busted his Kay.

Boom! Boom! Boom! Boom!

The other jacker ran in zig zags, and after a full minute, he evaded Rondo. Rondo jogged back to his truck with his pants around the back of his knees. He pulled them up as best he could. He handed the Draco to Skyy, got in, and pulled off.

***

After washing up in the hotel sink and breaking down the Draco, Rondo bleached and pissed on his hands to rid them of the gunpowder. He left and disposed of the assault rifles, then came back and was surprised when Skyy invited him back inside of her room. He strolled inside and sat on the couch with his mind racing.

"Say, shawty, I already know that dude's bitch ass put his hands on you. You already know that when yo' brother finds out that he finna crush that nigga. I hope he gives me that order though. I'ma shred that pussy."

Skyy grabbed a bottle of water out of the mini refrigerator and handed it to him. "You don't know if he did this or not, and even if he did, I know how to handle myself." She sat across from him on the edge of her bed.

Rondo looked her over. "Man, just knowing dat you trying to save dat nigga is enough to piss me the fuck off. Any nigga that needs to put his hand on a bitch deserves to be smoked. Fuck Gunnah. Blood living on borrowed time anyway."

Skyy smiled and got up. She sat beside him on the couch. "Damn, Rondo, you acting like you're mad because you thank he roughed me up and all of dat. Kinda seem like you care 'bout me and thangs."

Rondo looked off. “My heart is an ice box, shawty. Don't get shit twisted.”

Skyy smirked. “Yeah, right. Boy, don't let me find out dat you got a crush on me. Jimmy’ll whoop yo’ ass.” She pushed his shoulder.

“Shawty, I might be younger den most, but one thang is for sho, and dat’s dat I'm too much of a boss to have a crush on a bitch. I just don't thank a nigga should be putting his hands on a sister of one of the biggest Cartel members in da game.”

Skyy flared her nostrils and became angry. “I thought it was more den dat. Kinda liked the idea of you feeling me enough to wanna stank an opp over me. Now you talking all like dis done pretty much ruined the feeling I was feeling.” She rolled her eyes and was about to get up.

Rondo grabbed her arm and pulled her back down. “Damn Skyy, why you gotta make a nigga feel all soft and shit? You already know that you killing shit and that I'm feeling you. You just always gotta try and shit on me for no reason, is how I feel.”

Skyy sat back down. She saw promise within Rondo and wondered if she could run her game to get him to do her dirty work with Gunnah before Jimmy Bands gave the order to have him killed. She reached over and squeezed Rondo's thigh. “Only reason I be fronting like that is because I'm afraid of what my brother would do if he actually knew that I liked you a whole lot. Besides that, you and Jimmy got so many hoes I don't know where I would even fit in at. But I do like you, and I wanna know what's really good wit’ us? Thank you can handle an older woman like me?

Rondo smacked his lips. “Shawty, you only a year older den me as of yesterday. Besides all of dat, I get it out the mud, and I stand on my own two feet. I might ain't got the pull like Gunnah, but I'll smoke dat nigga and take dat shit from him for you. I'm just trying to see what's good wit' us. What you thanking?"

Skyy stood in front of him. "And you ain't scared of what Jimmy'll thank if he finds out?"

Rondo rubbed her exposed thighs. His hand ventured between her legs and cuffed her pussy. She moaned. "Hell nawl, I ain't. You gon' bless me right now though?"

Skyy licked her lips, and looked seductively at him. "What type of blessing is you talking 'bout?" she asked, playing coy. She wanted to see just how much heart Rondo really had.

Rondo stood up and wrapped his arms around her waist and gripped her booty through the small boy shorts that she was wearing. "I been wanting to get up with you, shawty, ever since the first day yo' brother introduced me to yo' fine ass. I don't mean to be basing you up or no shit like dat, but on everythang, you da baddest bitch I done ever seen in person. Ma'fucka like me won't have no problem cashing you. Dat's da real is what dat is right durr."

Skyy was flattered. She knew she was a looker, but the way Rondo was talking he made her feel like she was the hottest thing smoking. "Damn, Rondo, I ain't know you been feeling a way 'bout me. You sho' got a funny way of showing it." She stepped into his face. "I'm saying, shawty, do you kiss? Or are you like my brother and you don't trust where a female's lips have been?"

Rondo kissed her lips and licked all over them. He pulled his head back. "Dat answer dat question for you?"

Skyy smiled. So he trusted her. She liked that. Then she immediately felt like shit after remembering that less than an hour ago, she'd been made to give Gunnah head. She cursed herself and understood now why Jimmy Bands didn't allow for any female to kiss his lips. He felt that all of them were shiesty and up to no good, no matter what they proclaimed.

She rubbed his chest. "Check dis out, Rondo. Tonight I just want you to hold me while we sleep, and I want you to just listen to my heart. If you can get through dis night on dat level wit' me, den I promise da next time we link up dat it can be all 'bout you. Pending I ain't on my period or nothin' like dat."

"Damn, shawty, dat what da issue is dis time or somethin'?" He was disappointed and didn't know if he could simply lay in the bed with her without actually doing something to her gorgeous body. Then on top of that, the last he wanted to do was to listen to her heart. In truth, he didn't wanna do nothing less than fuck her, and nothing more. After all, he was still a boss member of the Duffle Bag Cartel.

"Nawl, li'l one, it ain't got nothin' to do wit' my cycle. It's just after that fuck boy Gunnah tried to force himself on me and all dat tonight, as much as I'm feeling you, sex is just da last thang on my brain. But I can already promise you dat da next time it won't be like dis. I'ma be 'bout whatever you 'bout however you 'bout it too."

Rondo raised his right eyebrow. "Yeah? So even if I wanna Orange Mound dis ass, you gon' let me blaze it?" He opened her cheeks and rolled his finger around her rose bud.

Skyy licked her juicy lips. "I don't know 'bout all dat, but let's just say nearly anythang else'll be on the table. Sound good to you?"

Rondo kissed her lips again and tried to slip his tongue into her mouth, but she creased her lips and prevented him from doing so. This irritated him. He backed up. "Yeah, whatever den. We still gon' blow this Kush doe, right? You know, before we get all into your emotions and shit?" He pulled out a box of already-rolled Dutch Masters.

Skyy laughed. "Yeah, dat's cool. And don't worry. I ain't gon' get too emotional on ya ass. I just want you to hear a few proposals I wanna drop in your lap on some serious get money schemes. After dat, we can breeze."

Rondo nodded. "Cool, let's get to it." He plopped on the couch and sparked his first of many blunts.

Chapter 15

"Rise and shine, Daddy. Open them brown eyes and greet the day," Natalia sang in her most cheerful voice.

Taurus opened his eyes and stretched his muscles. He scooted back in the bed until his back was against the headboard. Once there he closed his eyes, and yawned again. "Damn, what time is it?"

"It's just after one in the afternoon, and I've already touched base with Phoenix and told him that we are going to need another day." She straddled his lap and rested her hand on his shoulders. "So Daddy, I had time to sleep on what you told me to sleep on, and you said that whatever I was feeling when I woke up that you were going to be about. Well, I want you." She batted her long eyelashes flashing her crystal blue eyes that she'd inherited from her Russian mother.

"What? Nawl baby. I just knew that the guilt was going to get the better of you. What we did last night, you know playing around and shit was already out of order. I should have never crossed those lines with you. I'm your pops and I'm supposed to love you the right way."

Natalia was frozen with anger for a moment. She glared at Taurus and took a deep breath. "Who are you, or anybody else, to tell me how I want to be loved, or how I need to be loved? I am twenty-three years old. I know what I need from my father, and I know what will make me feel like a princess."

"Natalia, I'm telling you that right now, you're simply barking up my tree because of what's going on inside of you DNA-wise. But you gotta fight that, baby, because it's not right."

Natalia shook her head. "Screw that, Daddy. I have wanted you my whole life. I know it's crazy, and I know technically I'm not supposed to want you, but fuck that."

"Shawty, watch yo' mouth."

"Nawl, F that. My whole life I've been with men that wanted to sex me because of how good I looked, or how they imagined I would be in the sack, and with a few of them, I gave in because I was so naïve. I didn't stop to think one time that none of them cared about me, or didn't any of them mean a damn thing to me. That includes Phoenix to an extent because the only reason I fell for him in the forbidden way that I did is because I thought that he was the final male that I would ever have any connections to from our bloodline. I thought you were dead, Daddy. I thought that Phoenix was going to be as close as I could ever get to you. But he's not, because you're right here, and I need you. And I'm not taking no for an answer." She slid her hand down and inside of his boxer hole. Because he'd just woken up, his dick was already semi-hard. With the gripping of her small hand it rose and began to throb. She pulled it out of his boxers and began to pump it. "Look how you respond to me, Daddy." She stroked him faster and kissed the top of the head.

Taurus moaned under his breath. He closed his eyes and then opened them to see her small yellow hand wrapped around his piece stroking him. She was wearing a loose-fitting robe. Her breasts slowly began to sneak out of them, the nipples hard as calculus. "Damn, baby, if we do this, you can't hold dis shit against me. Please, 'cause I love you with all that I am as a man. Please don't hold it over my head."

Natalia went to her knees in a sixty-nine fashion. Her robe sailed above her waist to reveal her naked, shaven pussy lips. She arched her back and spaced her knees. In doing so, her pussy lips slightly parted. "I am you, Daddy. I'm the one baby girl that came out just like yo' ass. You did this wit yo' moms, and now I'm doing it wit' you. This is us, and this is what it is." She pulled back the skin of his piece and sucked it into her mouth, gobbling him.

Taurus moaned and placed his fingers into her curly hair. He guided her up and down his dick while he humped into her mouth from the big bed. “I ain't gon' take it easy on you, Natalia. Uhhh, fuck. I swear I ain't gon' take it easy on you. Yo’ Daddy is a savage in dese sheets. You finna find dat shit out the hard way.” He balled his fingers into her hair and forced her to take all of his pipe.

Natalia gagged and had to catch her breath. He pushed her down further and she held her breath while she sucked faster and harder. His piece reached the back of her throat and made her eyes water. She loved it. She let him guide her. “Ack. Ack. Ack. Ack.” Slurp. Slurp. Slurp. Slurp. Her head began to bob naturally in his lap.

Taurus rubbed her pussy and allowed for her to climb over his face. As soon as her pussy lined up with his mouth, he pulled her down and her bald lips came into contact with his tongue. He couldn't believe what they were doing, but it was already too late. He figured that he would live in the moment and just enjoy their time together because whether he did or not, it was happening. He opened her up and proceeded to make oral love to her gap in a way that he knew would drive her out of her mind.

Natalia sat straight up and began to ride his face, moaning loudly. “Daddy! Daddy! Daddy! Dis yo’ pussy! Dis yours, Daddy! Since day one. Uhhhh, shit, since day one!” she screamed, bouncing up and down on his tongue.

Taurus not only concentrated on her pussy, but he licked her ass and trapped her clit with his tongue. He manipulated her clitoris so much that she lost her breath when her orgasm began to rip through her worse than ever. She dug her nails into his thighs and threw her head back, cumming back to back. “Uhhhh, fuck! Uhhhh, fuck, Daddy!” she screamed.

Taurus slid from under her and forced her knees to her chest. He kept eating her, licking up and down her slit until she was trying to break away from him. He kept her trapped and brought her to two more orgasms with her knees pinned to her shoulders.

When she kicked out, she landed on her back and he was sure she would be exhausted. He crawled beside her like a hungry lion and sniffed her box. He growled and planted kisses all over it. Then he took a hold of her and flipped her on her stomach. He forced her knees to her chest and slipped deep into her pussy.

"You wanted Daddy? You got him." He pumped as hard as he could, slapping her on the side of the ass until it turned a shade of red. "You wanted yo' Daddy, right?"

"Yes! Daddy! Oooh! Finally! Fuck me! Fuck me! Fuck yo' baby girl, Daddy! Awww, damn!" She closed her eyes as he pounded into her. She could feel her ass cheeks jiggling every time he crashed into her. She struggled to get on her knees. As soon as she was there, she forced herself backward so she could take all of him again and again. Her face laid on the bed. He smacked her ass and pulled her long hair. She yelped. "Daddy, oooh, shit!"

Taurus was in a zone. He plunged deeper and deeper. He couldn't believe how tight she was, and wet. It seemed like the deeper he went the better the pussy got until she was shivering and cumming all over him. He smacked her ass and pulled all the way out. He leaned his face back into her box and sucked solely on her clitoris for three full minutes. She came again and fell on her stomach. He flipped her over and placed her thighs on his chest, slipped back in, and fucked her like a savage for a full thirty minutes without ceasing.

The dick became so good that Natalia began crying in ecstasy. "I love my Daddy. I love you so much, Daddy. Aw fuck, you turning me out. You turning me out, Daddy." She placed her fingers between her thighs to feel him going in and out of her better. Then she fell back and allowed for him to fuck her senselessly for another twenty minutes while she moaned and screamed his name.

Taurus picked up speed, looking into her eyes. He gripped her tighter and fucked harder. "I'm finna cum, baby. Daddy finna cum. Oooh, shit. My baby girl! My ma'fuckin' baby girl. Fuck, I hate myself for dis." He pounded into her with all of his might three hard times and pulled out. He pumped his piece as fast as he could and came all over her breasts and stomach in thick ropes. It spewed out of him and kept coming and coming. His abs locked up, and finally, he finished.

Natalia took a hold of his piece and sucked it into her mouth hungrily. She speared her head into his lap, moaning all around him. When she was sure that no more of him was going to come out, she rubbed him all over her face and collapsed to the bed, breathing hard.

Taurus fell beside her, breathing just as heavy. He looked over at her. "You still love yo' daddy, girl?"

Natalia forced herself to roll over and straddle him again. She laid her head on his chest. "I love you even more now, Daddy. Please don't love nobody else more than me. I don't think I will ever be able to handle that." She closed her eyes and drifted off to sleep, completely depleted.

Taurus's mind began to wander. Once again, he had failed himself. How could he have allowed for himself to slip into temptation the way that he had? He felt sick and weak. "Damn, here we go again," were his last words before he drifted off to sleep, angry at himself.

***

"Daddy? Daddy, wake up! You're tossing and turning and it's freaking me out." Natalia pushed on Taurus's chest again.

Taurus woke up with a start. He took a deep breath and sat straight up. Sweat slid down the side of his face. He wiped it away. "Natalia, baby, please tell me that we ain't crossed that line like I'm thanking we did? Tell me that it was all a dream." His chest heaved up and down rapidly.

Natalia frowned at him. "Daddy, what are you talking about? You said that today, after we woke up, that we would talk about it. I've been sitting here waiting for you to wake up this whole time. Impatient, to be honest with you." She rubbed his chest and dared to lay a kiss on it.

"So you mean that we didn't go all the way? Is that what you're saying?"

Natalia smiled seductively. "What if we did? It's too late to take it back now." She climbed on top of him and peeled back her short silk robe. Her breasts bared and bounced out for his view. She leaned forward and kissed both sides of his cheeks. "All I've ever wanted was my daddy, and I got him. I ain't never felt this whole in my entire life." She turned her head sideways and laid it on his chest.

Taurus laid there for a minute and then he eased from under her, at a loss for words. He stood at the side of the bed in just a pair of boxers that allowed for his piece to swing from side to side. " Natalia, I'm sorry, baby."

"For what, Daddy? You didn't do anything that I didn't beg for you to do. I don't want you feeling like you've hurt me in any way, because you haven't. All of those scumbag Russians that my mother brought home under the guise of them being her boyfriend, or some sort of distant relative to me, that actually took advantage of me, they are the ones that hurt me - not you. You love me, and I am nuts over you, and I have been yearning for you in this way my entire life. Now, Daddy..."

She crawled across the bed on her knees sexily. She stopped in front of him at the edge of the bed and pulled him to her. "Daddy, nobody will ever find out about this. Until the day that I die, this will be our secret. I love you for giving in to me, and now I know what it's like to be with you, to be with the man that so many women and men have revered. It was everything." Her big blue eyes peered into his.

"I'm still at a loss for words, baby. I should have been stronger. It's just that you're so damn fine, and we came into each other's lives when you were already looking like this. Then your father ain't been with a woman in nearly two years, and my head is so fucked up, then the drank we was sipping, and the smoke we blew. None of it helped this cause. I regret it, and I feel like a fuck nigga because I surrendered to my baby."

"Well, you shouldn't. It's like I said before, I know how I want and need to be loved by and from you. This is how." She rubbed her face against his. "To me, this is the perfect love. I understand why every female that crosses your path needs this from you. I get it now." She moved back so she could look into his eyes. "Daddy, all I ask is that you continue to build me up. Keep telling me how beautiful I am. How strong, and what I mean to you. Though I may be tough, I still need to know that I am your little girl, and that I am special. This bond that we have, this love isn't so unfamiliar to other people within our position. I envied two of my best friends because they shared this same love with their dads. I was the only one that knew, and I was so jealous because they were so spoiled, and so loved." She shook her head. "But anyway, it's okay. I am thankful for you. So chill. We're good." She held his shoulders and kissed his lips. "And now we have to get this pandemic in order. There are some things that I wanna run by you that is going to turn the White House upside down. All I ask is that you listen to me, and allow your baby girl to do what she does best. How does that sound?" Her hands dared to run over his tattooed chest.

Taurus took a deep breath and exhaled, looking into her eyes. "Shawty, you so much like me that it's scary. I ain't got no other choice other than to hear you out. So, let's roll."

Chapter 16

"One hunnit, two hunnit, three hunnit, four hunnit, five hunnit, six hunnit, seven, eight, nine hunnit thousand right here. You got another hunnit over durr. Dat's all we need. Here you go, playboy. Now let me see dat artillery shit dat you been boasting 'bout," Jimmy Bands said as he slid the piles of taped cash across the huge table to Rivera.

Rivera was a coldhearted drug lord that operated under the Sinaloa Cartel out of Mexico City, Mexico. He was ruthless and touted to be a superior boss. He dealt solely with the inner cities that were infested with struggling Blacks and Latinos across the United States and all the way down to South America. After some serious urging by Phoenix, Rivera had finally been convinced to do business with the Duffle Bag Cartel out of fear that if he did not, he would lose out on a significant amount of money, and he was sure that it would wind up going to one of his rivals. That wouldn't look good to the few bosses that sat above him. There was a major war coming between the Duffle Bag Cartel that controlled the drug supply throughout the trenches of Tennessee, Arizona, and Texas, and the Bread Gang, that controlled the music industry by way of a few powerful drug lords that had their monies tied up in investments with a few of the talents that were a part of the new label. The Bread Gang was not only a series of rappers and R&B stars, but they were also trap stars in the streets, and had a variety of dope boys that polarized the gang's name and had reinvented it into that of a money-getting cartel that spanned from Memphis to Atlanta and everywhere in between. Now that the Bread Gang had control of millions of dollars because of the music industry, they were serious about reinvesting their monies into life narcotics. That's where Rivera came in at, and that's where he looked to capitalize off of both sides.

You see, when it came to the Game, a true drug lord didn't care about how he made his money. He didn't care about who got hurt, or who he had to hurt in order to continue to constantly remain on the top of the mountain of kingpins. As long as the money was good and plentiful, he played however many sides as he had to. The fact of the matter was that both the Duffle Bag Cartel and the Bread Gang were nothing more than mere peasants in the grand scheme of things. Whenever one was annihilated, the powers above would do nothing more than invest inside of another up and coming crew that would rival whichever crew had withstood the war previously. The goal was to keep a money-getting gang of Blacks and Latinos to remain in the view of the disenfranchised people of their communities. Their false stature gave their people hope and the false ideation that drug selling, murder, guns, and narcotics was the way of life, and the only way that they could rise out of the abyss of the ghetto. In reality, it was nothing more than a game and a ruse for the prison systems to remain overpopulated, and the two dominant races, Blacks and Latinos, to remain chained down and trapped in the system. But no matter what the overall goal was, Rivera was going to play the middle because it had him chasing a billion dollars in cold hard cash.

Rivera was dressed in a three piece black and white suit with his thick, black, wavy hair slicked backward. He raised his right hand into the air and snapped his fingers. As soon as he did, the black Hummer that was parked at the back of the warehouse started and drove forward. It stopped in front of Rivera and five men jumped out. They stood behind him in army fatigues. The driver handed the keys to Rivera and stood in place alongside the rest of his crew.

Rivera took the keys and handed them to Jimmy Bands. "Inside the Hummer is a collection of some of the deadliest military issued assault rifles and automatic handguns, worth more than a million dollars. There are also explosives, and a variety of other devices that will turn any war upside down. You make sure that you tell Phoenix that I send my regard."

Jimmy Bands felt a level of jealousy for a moment. "I'll make sure dat I do exactly dat." He gave Rondo the nod to watch his back for a moment. Rondo winked, and then Jimmy Bands went inside of the Hummer and unzipped one of the US Army leather Duffle bags. He pulled out a MP90 and stepped back out of the Hummer. He looked the weapon over and nodded his head. "What dis bitch do right hurr?"

"Shoots a hundred and fifty rounds rapidly. Ninety-eight percent accurate from a hundred yards or less. More than that, it drops to seventy-five. There is a cooling system, and the scope is in HD in case you wanna shoot a man's pimple off of his face," Rivera continued. "There are ten of them in there, and these bad boys are what helped the United States win the war in Kosovo."

"Dat's what I'm talking about right dere, homie. What are the odds dat we are the only crew on da streets with dese?" Jimmy Bands eyed Rivera closely.

"Everything for me is business. Just like you serve the best of the best narcotics, I sell the best of the best arms around the country. But it is best that you have these in your arsenal over or just as well as anybody else. Our job here is done." Rivera twirled his finger in a circle and gave the order for his men to file out.

Jimmy Bands felt disrespected. The meeting hadn't ended, as far as he was concerned, and Rivera's abrupt attempt to end it irritated him. "Word on da street is dat you are standing behind the Bread Gang. Dat true?"

Rivera jacked his coat and turned around to address Jimmy Bands. “Excuse me?”

“You heard what I said, homeboy. I said, word in the trenches say dat your Cartel is fully invested in the Bread Gang, even doe you know dat da Bread Gang is the Duffle Bag Cartel's first rival. Seems like it should be a conflict of interest to you and you should have to pick sides, seeing as we done put millions in yo’ pocket already.”

Rivera stepped as close to Jimmy Bands as he could without actually touching him or getting either side of killas on edge. “Since when are you the cabron that's going to tell me who to do business with? Case you didn't know, my business is mine and mine only. You got your shipment. Our business is done.” He turned to walk away again.

“A friend of my enemy is also my enemy, but a friend of mine can potentially be my enemy’s worst nightmare,” Jimmy Bands uttered.

Rivera turned around again. “What the fuck is that supposed to mean?”

Jimmy Bands sneered at him. “What's it gon' take to get you to drop dem and cross solely over to the Duffle Bag Cartel? I am sure that whatever it will take that we as a unit can make it happen.”

Rivera laughed. “Son, our business is done. Before you or anybody can lock down the powers in Mexico, you need to at first reach a billion dollars. In case you didn't know, your President lives in the White House with access to trillions of dollars, and we don't even submit to him. He lives there, yet we control the country and the powers that be. The sooner you learn that you are nothing more than a pawn in this game of masters, the sooner you will be thankful that you still have breath in your lungs. Our business is concluded. Vamanos!” He twirled his finger in a circle again, and his troops loaded up, ready to file out. "The Hummer is yours. You're welcome." He laughed again before they departed from the warehouse.

Jimmy Bands stood there for a long time with his savage crew of thirty behind him. He nodded his head and cursed under his breath. He was tired of being treated like a low level nobody. If this was the game that Rivera wanted to play, he would master it as a man and make him pay for his sins. "Let's get the fuck up out of here, mane! Now!"

***

Gunnah hopped out of his 1964 Chevy Impala and slammed the door behind him. He had two forty Glocks tucked on each side of his waist, and a bulletproof vest across his chest. Behind him were two of his loyal Orange Mound killas that were looking forward to moving up the ladder of the slums that Gunnah currently had within his grasp. Gunnah pulled the door open to Flawless Beauty hair salon and walked inside with his troops behind him.

The salon was set up to give each person inside their own space for social distancing. Each salon chair was divided by plexiglass glass, and the stylist that worked the section had on a 3M doctor's mask and made sure that they kept their section clean and sterilized to the best of their abilities.

When Gunnah walked inside, all of the females inside stopped what they were doing and turned to look at him. The shop was packed above the recommended safe capacity for social distancing. Gunnah walked up to one of the beauticians, a short, caramel, heavyset sister with a beautiful face, and stood in front of her. "Say, shawty, where Skyy's ass at?"

The beautician rolled her eyes and ignored him. She knew Gunnah quite well and she knew that he was a lowlife dog.

His status was new, and not everybody got the memo - her being one of them. She continued to do the little girl's hair that sat in her chair.

Gunnah cleared his throat. “Shawty, you heard what I asked yo’ ass? Where dat Skyy girl at? I need to talk to her?”

She frowned. “She got social media accounts and a phone. If she wanted to talk to yo’ dog ass, I'm sho' she'd hit you up. Dang, quit being a bug.” She scrunched her nose and tried to ignore his ugly face again.

Gunnah was taken aback. “Fuck you just say?”

The beautician rolled her eyes and shook her head. “Damn, are you really dat oblivious?”

Gunnah laughed. “Yeah, every day I gotta remind ma’fuckas who run da Mound.” He upped his gun and pressed it to her forehead. The other females in the shop screamed and dropped to the floor. The door was blocked by his goons, so they were unable to run out of the door. “You wanna rephrase dat shit?”

The beautician looked him directly in the eyes, fearless. “I ain't scared of nobody but Jesus Christ. Seeing as you ain't got no holes in your hands or your feet, you don't scare me one fucking lick. You wanna kill me, then bury me as a child of God and saturated within the blood of Christ.”

“Bitch, what?” He cocked the hammer, ready to off her with no hesitation.

“You heard what I said. Satan, get thee behind me in the mighty name of Jesus.”

“Yeah, awright.” He swung the gun and smacked her so hard across the face that he knocked her out cold. She landed on her stomach with blood leaking out of her forehead. He stomped her in the back. “Punk-ass bitch. I am Satan. Now somebody better tell me where the fuck Skyy is, or I'm finna kill everybody in here, including this crying li'l bitch right here." He grabbed the six-year-old girl whose hair the beautician had been and picked her up in the air by her throat. He slung her across the room. She landed on the floor with the wind knocked out of her.

"She not here!" a light skinned, chubby female yelled with her head covered.

Gunnah stepped over to her and picked her up by her hair. She screamed and tried to get him to cut her loose, to no avail. Gunnah pressed his gun to her eye. "Where the fuck she at den?"

"I don't know. She was here earlier, and she left in a red Jaguar. That was the last time that I saw her."

Gunnah dropped her to the floor. He mugged her and tried to calm down. "Who da fuck drive a red Jaguar? Dat must be dat nigga Jimmy Bands' shit." He grew angry. "Listen up. Y'all betta get on line and reach out to dat bitch and tell her to check in wit' me. Don't none of my hoes go more than twelve hours without checking in wit' a boss. Dis is a new day, and dis how we running shit. She wanna play wit' me, den I'ma take dat shit out on you hoes. Got it?" he roared, still wondering how Skyy could have enough gall to not return his calls.

Most would think that a man going this far over a female not returning his calls or texts was excessive, but most had never run across a possessive, chauvinistic, egotistical, low life, no value-having heathen like Gunnah, who was power drunk. He was secretly madly in love with Skyy, and he got off on possessing her in every single way imaginable, especially since he was paying all of her bills.

"You hoes pass my message and make it lighter on yourselves. Sniper Gang out." He turned and left with his crew.

***

Rondo set a duffle bag on the bed of the hotel room and dug out twenty thousand dollars. He thumbed the money for a moment, and then handed the knot over to Skyy. “Hurr, boo, dis a li'l chump change for a bad bitch. You thank it’ll be enough to last you for the week?”

Skyy looked over the money and wanted to smile bright. They had only been talking for a week, and already, Rondo had been cashing her more than any other man that she’d ever been with, and she was finding it hard to contain herself. “How much is dis right hurr?”

“It's just twenty thousand. Shit light. I know dat nigga Gunnah be hitting you, but for right now, this gon' have to suffice. I'ma get you right some more, but I just had to hit you with something until I get to where I need to be after we buss this move later.”

Skyy tucked the money in her purse and set the purse on the couch. “I mean, I'm used to getting hit like that damn near every day,” she lied, “but this is definitely a start. I see how you're coming for me. I appreciate you, baby.” She pulled him to her and kissed his lips.

“It’s all good. I know dat nigga can't fuck wit’ my bidness. I just wanna show you dat. Dat way you don't get to regretting crossing over to a nigga. After I buss his head tonight, everything gon' be in motion. Bet that.”

“I know it will be, baby. I just want us to be rocking wit’ the best of everything. Ain't no such thang as us parading round Memphis if we gon' be broke. My brother has all dat money and thangs, and you just barely making it. I don't understand how all dat dope shit work and all dat, but if I was in the mob, I'd make sho’ I was taken care of on a whole ’nother level.” She licked the side of his neck. “Every nigga should strive to be a king, and not a worker. You feel me?”

Rondo grew angry. “Damn, so you thank I'm broke or some shit? Why you fucking wit’ me den?”

Skyy had to continue to bruise his ego to get him where she needed him to be. She had a plan in place inside of her mind that she needed to finesse through Rondo. He was young, naïve, and prideful. That was perfect for her. She kissed his lips again. “Nawl, li'l daddy, don't go getting all defensive and shit. It is what it is. First thang you gotta know ’bout me is dat I'm a straight shooter. I ain't gon' blow smoke up yo’ ass unless you into that.” She winked at him.

Rondo dismissed her. “Fuck is you saying, Shawty?”

Skyy laughed and grew serious. “Guess what I'm saying is that you got potential, but you ain't really on shit. You got a few thousand, and that doesn't mean shit. Nigga, dat’s bill money. Twenty G’s is going out on the town money. Once I buy an outfit and get my hair and nails done, buy some earrings, and pay for our meals at one of the restaurants that I like to go to, I'ma be back broke. So while I understand what you are trying to do, you really ain't on shit. Not that level that Jimmy and Gunnah is on.” She studied him.

“What? Bitch, you tripping. See, I was just giving you a little bit of nothin'. It’s already Wednesday, and I was gon' hit you again Friday with another twenty, but since you making me feel like a bum-ass nigga, nah.”

“Nawl baby, you ain't gotta give me nothing else. I know you ain't got it like that. Keep yo’ bread.” She smiled within.

“Man, shut the fuck up before I slap yo’ ass. Dis is me. I got this.” He dug inside of the bag and pulled out thirty more G’s. “Hurr, that's fifty. You should be good wit’ that, and if you ain't, you can kiss my ass.”

Skyy took the money. “But baby, I would've done that anyway.” She dropped the money on the bed.

"I ain't tripping because after I hit dude's bitch ass tonight, we gon' be good anyway. You sho' these are all the codes?"

"Yep. I worked my magic, and got them directly out of his phones. I'ma touch base with him tonight because he been blowing me up on some angry shit, and that's when it'll be smartest to buss your move."

"Our move. But I get what you saying. Fo' we do dat, I wanna buss you down. I'm loving da way dat pussy sitting right in dese pink boy shorts and I'ma tryna fuck something right now." He reached between her thighs and rubbed her pussy. It felt hot and chunky.

Skyy smiled. "I'ma tell you what. Let me shower and get my hygiene together. Soon as I'm done, I'ma let you do you. How does that sound?"

Rondo shook his head. "Fuck that. I wanna fuck that ass right now. I been wanting to put my dick in dat booty since the first time I saw how far it poked out from your lower back. Fuck that shower. We fucking right now. I already got the KY Jelly." He dug it out of his bag and held it up.

Skyy swallowed her spit and became nervous. "Damn, baby, you ain't gon' let me get clean first?"

Rondo set the Duffle bag on the floor and cleared off the bed. "Come here," He motioned with his finger.

Skyy shook her head. "Nawl, boy, we gon' do our thang afterwards.

Rondo walked toward her. "No we ain't. We finna fuck right now. Bring yo ass here."

"Ain't. Now you gon' wait li'l Daddy. I'll only be a minute." She turned to walk into the hotel's bathroom.

Rondo allowed for her to take five steps before he rushed her and tackled her to the floor. "You got me fucked up."

"Get off of me, boy! What the fuck is wrong with you?"

Rondo ripped her blouse down the middle and yanked her Victoria's Secret bra from her chest. Her titties spilled out into the open. He moaned at the sight of them. "Damn ,dem bitches pretty." He ripped her panties halfway off next. She kicked her legs, and he ignored her. He applied more force. "I been hitting you like a ma'fucka. You ain't 'bout to keep playing wit' me. I ain't as much of a goofy as you thank I am. I just got a weakness for you." He stripped her and turned her on her stomach. His knees were between hers. He grabbed the KY Jelly and squirt it all over her crack. Her juicy ass began to shine before his gaze.

"Don't do this, Rondo. I told you I just wanted to clean up first. Why you acting like you can't wait?"

Rondo greased up his dick and stroked it up and down. Skyy looked over her shoulder at how much meat he was working with and she grew nervous. She had never seen a dick so big in her life. She didn't feel that there was any way that she could take even half of him. Rondo squeezed her booty and groaned.

Skyy tried with no avail to free herself. "Please, Rondo."

Rondo was too busy laying on top of her back. He wiggled his big dick head from side to side. He found her heat and squirted a hefty portion of the jelly into her crack. He pushed inward and sank four inches. Her heat made him whimper.

Skyy closed her eyes and bit into her bottom lip. "Rondo, please. Stop. I can't take all dat. Please."

Rondo was too far gone. The Mollie and Percocets in his system had won the battle. He needed to feel her all the way. He had to. He cocked back and slammed forward, impaling all ten thick inches into her back door. "Awwww, fuck!"

Skyy grabbed at the carpet as she felt him begin to fuck her like an animal. "Shit! Shit! Shit! Aww! Rondo! Rondo! Oooh! Stop!"

Rondo grabbed her hips and fucked her hard and fast. He watched his dick disappear between her thick ass cheeks and it hyped him up. “Yeah! Yeah! Bitch! Gimme dis ass! Gimme dis shit. Uhhhhh! It’s so good. It’s so ma’fuckin’' good! Bounce dat shit back! Do it! Twerk on my shit!” He pulled her to her knees.

Skyy winced in both pain and pleasure. She arched her back and followed his orders. “Unnnn! Unnnn! Unnnn! Fuck Rondo, you're killing me!”

“Twerk, bitch!” He slapped her ass on the sides and fucked her harder. “Twerk!”

Skyy popped her juicy ass. It jiggled and shook over and over like Jell-O. She reached between her thighs and pinched her clit to send chills throughout her system. She moaned, and he went deeper. He slapped her ass over and over. Every smack drove her insane. Now she was rolling her clit in a circular motion. She arched her back and pinched her jewel again. “Rondo! Rondo! Ooooooooh!” She came harder, jerking and jerking, falling to her stomach while he continued to fuck her.

Rondo dug deeper. He bit into her neck as the reality that he was fucking Jimmy Bands' little sister came into his mind, and he came hollering at the top of his lungs deep inside of her ass. He came and came, biting all over her back. Then he collapsed on top of her, breathing hard, his piece throbbing inside of her back door. “Damn, that ma’fucka is every bit as good inside as it looks on the outside.” He slowly slipped his piece out and turned on his back.

Skyy crawled to her knees, looking down at him. She grabbed his pipe and squeezed it in her hand, even though she was heated and felt both betrayed and taken advantage of. This was Memphis. When it came down to the thugs here, it would have been stupid of her to expect any less than what she got. "You just had to have me, huh, baby?"

Rondo nodded. "You ma'fuckin' right. Now dat we got dat out of da way, you can start to honor da fact dat you my bitch. I ain't tryna be on no cuffing shit, but I know I better at least have da first stakes on dis ass. Dat's for sure."

"See , dat's what you fail to realize. I don't get down like dat. If I'm rocking wit Rondo, then I'm only rocking wit' Rondo. I am a one woman man, and I'm feeling you, so that's who I'm loyal too. You ain't gotta worry 'bout me fuckin' wit' nobody else. That's my word."

Rondo got up and stretched his arms over his head. "Dat shit sounds good. Either way, I ain't tripping. I'm feeling you and everythang like dat, but it's so many hoes in Memphis dat you gotta know dat you can't be my only one. Right now I'm focused solely on da money, but if shit change, I'ma do me." He looked her up and down and headed to the shower.

Skyy raised her right eyebrow. Now she was feeling a way. Before Rondo had fucked, he acted as if she had an easy chance of locking him down. But now that he'd gotten what he wanted, it seemed that things had changed dramatically. "Say, Rondo."

He stopped and turned to face her. His dick swung from side to side. "What up?"

"What, you ain't feeling me or something no more?" She walked up on him. "I mean what gives?"

Rondo frowned. "Hell yeah I am, shawty. You still a bad bitch. I just want us to set the record straight up front. I'm getting money. When you chase money, hoes come along with the game. When you chase hoes, money runs away from you. So I'ma keep chasing the money and let shit fall where it falls. But you're most definitely mine though." He grabbed her to him roughly and tongued her down for a full two minutes.

When he finished, he smacked her on the ass and went to shower.

Skyy stood in front of the closed shower door, irritated that he didn't allow for her to shower with him. She saw that he was too headstrong. She needed to break him quick and dispose of him. Time was of the essence.

Chapter 17

Phoenix eased into the kitchen and snuck up behind Jahliyah as she poured herself a hot cup of coffee. She wore a pair of barely-there white lace panties under a small beater that broadcast her nipples. Her robe hung open loosely, and her curly hair was still wet from the shower. Phoenix could smell the coconut scent of her. He slipped behind her and wrapped his arms around her small waist. She jumped, and his lips kissed her neck.

Jahliyah smelled his cologne and already knew who it was. He ground his front into her rounded ass. She popped him on the side. “Phoenix, I've been here going on eight days, and you've been on my heels every day that I've been here. I ain't going. When are you going to get that shit through your big head?”

Phoenix ground into her, rubbing his piece from side to side on his flimsy boxers. “Shawty, you da one walking round dis ma’fucka in damn near nothing. You can't knock me for wanting to be all over dis ass right hurr. I can't help it.” He sucked on her neck and scraped along her jugular with his teeth. His right hand dipped around and into her crease. He rubbed her gap until it was moist. He didn't know how or why, but he was starting to see that all of Taurus's daughter's had fat pussies. It was like a rite of passage, he guessed.

“What do you think my sister would say if she knew that her baby daddy had been feeling all over her sister ever since she’s been here? You think she'd be cool wit’ that?” She turned around until they were nose to nose.

Phoenix gripped her ass and slipped his fingers under the band of her panties until he was rubbing her naked pussy lips. “I don't know what she would say, and I already know dat you wouldn't tell her no damn way, so why are we even talking 'bout dat?" He opened her lips and slowly slipped his middle finger inside of her.

Jahliyah took a deep breath and closed her eyes. "Boy, you are tripping. Did you forget that you are my cousin?"

"Hell nawl, he didn't forget," Natalia said as she stepped into the kitchen and dropped her Gucci bag on the floor.

Phoenix broke away from Jahliyah and bucked his eyes at Natalia's presence. "Baby, damn, when did you get home?"

Natalia mugged and ignored him. "So you must be Jahliyah?"

Jahliyah could not believe how absolutely gorgeous Natalia was. The way her blue eyes popped on her golden skin, her long curly hair fell below her small waist, and her thick thighs molded to the Fendi dress she wore almost made her intimidated. "Damn, you're my little sister?"

"By four months." Natalia walked over and extended her hand. As enamored as Jahliyah was with her, she was equally enamored. Jahliyah's caramel skin was flawless. Her brown eyes shone, and her dimples were so deep on her cheeks that it made her look beyond gorgeous. Her body was immaculate. She was equally strapped in all the right places, and her hair was full of sheen. Natalia became jealous and prayed that Taurus wouldn't love her sister more than her. After all, she was his first daughter, and she looked just like the pictures of Princess that she'd seen. This worried her.

Jahliyah held her hand after shaking it. "I know that you walked up on yo' baby daddy all over me and stuff like that, but I just wanna let you know that we ain't didn't nothing while you was gone. Even though I don't really know you, you are still my sister and I would never betray you like—" Jahliyah stopped talking mid-sentence and nudged Natalia aside. She covered her face with both of her hands for a moment and then the tears started to sail down her cheeks. "Daddy, is that you?"

Taurus had stepped into the kitchen fitted in Chanel. His deep waves shone, and the shirt was tight enough to showcase his muscular physique. He dropped his bags and nodded his head. "Jahliyah, boo-boo, that's you?"

"Yes, Daddy." Now she was in full tears.

"Damn, you look just like your mother." He opened his arms. "Come here."

She took off running and jumped into his arms. Taurus picked her up and turned around and around in the kitchen with her. He held her by the bottom as if she was a little kid. He immediately felt the presence and spirit of Princess radiating through Jahliyah. It made him weak.

Natalia stood back, devastated. Already she hated their connection. Taurus hadn't spun her around or held her in the way that he was holding Jahliyah, and he was still holding her. This infuriated her even more. Hugs shouldn't last that long. *Has he already forgotten about me?* She wanted to cry. She stomped her right foot. "Okay, damn."

Phoenix stood back and appreciated how Jahliyah's panties were all up in her ass and exposing her cheeks. Taurus had her gripped just right, and he didn't even know it. Taurus felt like he was holding his newborn baby all over again. Phoenix was hard as a rock. He watched until Taurus lowered her, and then he slipped out of the kitchen.

Natalia forced her way in between the two of them and laid her head on Taurus's shoulders. Taurus wrapped his arm around her. Natalia mugged Jahliyah. "So now that you've seen him, how long are you going to be here?" She didn't mean to sound so rude, but he couldn't help it.

Jahliyah was shocked. "Well, I took a few weeks' vacation time from work. Had I known that the two of you were going to be gone for a week, I would have come later. But if it is an inconvenience with me staying here, I will surely make other arrangements."

"Cool." Natalia crossed her arms.

Taurus frowned down at her. "Natalia, stop that, li'l lady. You don't mean that."

"Well, you didn't see what her and Phoenix was doing before you came into the kitchen. I can't trust her around him, and look at how she's walking around somebody else's mansion. What type of shit is that?" She glared at her.

"Fine, if you want me out, then I'm out. I already apologized for what took place between Phoenix and myself, and I assure you that nothing happened. But, I'll be out of here in an hour." She hugged Taurus again and headed out of the kitchen.

"Jahliyah, stop." Taurus boomed.

Jahliyah stopped in her tracks. "Yes, Daddy?"

Taurus turned to Natalia. "Baby girl, I ain't never had my daughters under one roof. I have missed the both of y'all greatly and I want to get to know the both of you. So Jahliyah, you ain't going nowhere, and neither are you, Natalia. Jahliyah has one week before she has to return to New York, and we are all going to be a family until then. That's just that. You understand me, Natalia?"

Natalia shook her head and felt her throat tighten. "I guess, Daddy. D whatever y'all want." She walked out of the kitchen, and upstairs to her bedroom, hoping that Taurus would follow behind her. When he did not, she came back downstairs after ten minutes to locate him. She found him and Jahliyah hugging again. She ran back to her room full of tears and spite.

***

Later that night, Taurus knocked on Natalia's bedroom door. She was up brushing her hair at her vanity. "Who is it?" she called, lowering the brush.

"Daddy. Can I talk to you for a minute, baby?"

Natalia took a deep breath and blew it out. "It's open, Daddy."

Taurus opened the door and stepped inside. He closed it back and slipped beside Natalia on the bed. "Are you okay?"

Natalia jumped up and ran between his legs. She wrapped her arms around his neck. "You love her more than you do me, don't you, Daddy? Be honest; I can handle it. Wait a minute, no I can't. Just tell me what I need to do." She started to shake.

Taurus stood up and held her. "Baby, why are you freaking out?" He held her tightly and kissed the top of her head.

"Because she looks just like you, and I can tell that you are crazy about her. I don't know if I can take this."

"Natalia, baby, but I am crazy about you too. Both of you are my daughters and I would do anything for either one of you. You need to know that."

"I do, Daddy, but I don't want to share you. She already has your skin complexion, your eyes, your dimples, and her mother's name is tattooed on your chest. I don't have anything. It's not fair, and I have been looking for you my entire life. For God's sakes, I just gave the word for my people to infect the entire White House with a virus that they wanted you to use against your own people. Doesn't that count for anything?"

Taurus grew impatient. "Baby, ain't no reason for you to feel intimidated by Jahliyah. She is your sister, and she loves you, as do I. We are a family, and I will never turn my back on you, or choose anybody over you. Our love is pure and strong. I promise." He hugged her tighter and kissed her forehead again.

Natalia shivered. She took a step back and rushed to lock the door. “Five minutes then, Daddy, please, just make love to me for five minutes so my heart can be put at ease. Please, nobody will hear I just need you so bad.” She hurried over to him and cuffed his piece.

“Noooo, baby, come on now.” Taurus removed her hands from him. He held them. “We're good. You are my life and we don't need to screw every time you think that you are losing me. I love you, and Daddy ain't going nowhere, I promise. Now come here and let me hold you.”

Natalia flopped on the bed. “I don't want to be held by you, Daddy. I need you to make love to me. You just held Jahliyah. The only way we can set the two relationships apart is to make love again.” She lowered her hands to her face and broke down.

Taurus sighed and dropped his head. He came over and rested his head on her thighs. “Baby, besides that, what can Daddy do to let you know that you are my world and that I ain't choosing nobody over you?”

Natalia shrugged her shoulders. “I just want you. I don't understand why I gotta share you with Jahliyah. She had all these years to track you down like I did, but she never took the initiative. That should tell you right there who loves you the most. Damn, doesn't she have a whole brother that she can love up on? All I got is you.” Natalia held him on to him for dear life.

“Damn, baby, that's why I feel like we shouldn't have done anything with each other on that physical level. I know our DNA, and whenever a man in our family does something with a woman of our bloodline, it never ends well. It always ends in tragedy. I could have avoided that. Fuck.”

Natalia held him for a moment longer. “That is not the response that I was expecting to hear from you.” She sighed and released him. She turned away from him and walked to the door in her room and opened it, ready to leave so she could take a drive and get some fresh air. "Maybe I am doing too much. I mean, after all, you are my father. I shouldn't feel intimidated by my sister, even though I can't help but to admit that she is gorgeous." She shook her head in remembering how Jahliyah looked with Phoenix all over her. That angered her. "Daddy, are you sure that the bond that you and I have will never be shared or broken up by Jahliyah, or anybody else?"

Taurus nodded. "Come here, baby. Into these arms." He held them open for her.

Natalia slowly turned around and strolled into his arms with a look of depression written all over her face. When she felt his arms secure her, she grew even weaker. "Daddy, I don't like this feeling. You need to answer me."

Taurus held her beautiful face within his big hands and looked into her blue eyes. "Listen to me, Natalia."

"Baby, I like it when you call me your baby. So call me that. Please."

Taurus smiled. "Baby, listen to me, there is nothing or no one that could ever break up or share our bond. I am not looking to cross those boundaries with Jahliyah, and I shouldn't have crossed them with you, but what's done is done."

"You didn't have a choice when it came to me. I would have never let up until you gave me what I have always wanted from you, but I see what you're saying though. Go on."

"Baby, what you and I have is special, and rare. Our bond will not, and can not, be broken. Your daddy loves you with all of his heart, and I got you. Now come here."

Natalia hugged his neck and kissed all over his lips. Her tongue darted into his mouth and found his. She moaned and melted into him more and more. “I just love you so much, Daddy, I can't help myself.”

Taurus broke the kiss and wiped his lips. “I know, li'l baby, and you never will. Daddy promises you that.”

“And I believe you. That's all I needed to hear, Daddy. I swear it is.”

***

Jahliyah stood outside of the door with Phoenix standing next to her. She was perplexed and a bit confused. She was sure that Natalia was her blood sister through Taurus, and if that was the case, she didn't understand how they could have made out the way that they had. She also wondered if it went further than that. She was angry and turned off. She walked away from the door.

Phoenix shook his head in anger. He felt he should have known. His whole life he'd heard about the forbidden legacy of Taurus and how he got down long before he himself was even born. So to witness him screwing with Natalia didn't shock or surprise him. It was what it was. He simply felt betrayed by Natalia and he wanted to seek his revenge, knowing that it was more than likely that the week that she and Taurus had spent together was full of sex and all things taboo. *Punk bitch,* he thought. A major part of him was tired of living inside of Taurus's legacy. He wanted to create his own legacy, and in order for him to be able to do just that, he would have to crush his uncle once and for all, and in the midst of smashing him, take over his multimillion dollar drug infrastructure. Phoenix pulled his nose and slipped from the crack of the doorway with snake in his blood and double crossing on his mind.

Chapter 18

The doorbell rang.

Skyy fluffed her hair behind her ears and looked over her shoulders to make sure that nobody was getting ready to run up on her. She had already spotted Gunnah's Benz truck parked inside of his driveway, so she knew he was home. The girls at the shop had already told her how he'd come looking for her with a vengeance. She was nervous that he was about to get real physical with her, but she simply hoped that he wouldn't kill her. As long as he didn't do that, she would be good, she prayed.

When Gunnah came to the door and looked out of it, he spotted Skyy and his anger began to surge through him. He tossed open the screen door, pulling his belt through the loops of his pants.

“Well, well, well, look who it is. You already know yo ass is in trouble, don't you?”

Skyy shifted from one foot to the next. “I heard you was looking for me and all of that, but—”

Gunnah grabbed a handful of her hair and slung her inside of his residence. “Bitch, shut the fuck up! Everybody out, right now!”

The house was packed with three of his dope boys counting up the week's take, two security guards that were watching them count his paper, and four females that Gunnah was going to make perform for him that night. At the sight of Skyy, he wanted to be alone. He had some things in mind for her that he would be embarrassed if anybody else saw. He waited until all of them left before he slammed the door.

Skyy scooted backward on her ass. She stopped when her back hit the wall. She rubbed the spot in her head where Gunnah had torn a few roots. “Gunnah, before you get on my ass,

I need you to know that I didn't do anything wrong. I was in jail. My brother was supposed to come bail me out," she lied, "but he took his sweet time. It wasn't my fault. Then I didn't wanna call you from no fuckin' jail phone. You would have tried to kill me 'bout dat, so I didn't know what to do, but I'm here now." She looked up at him, worried about coming to her feet from fear that he wouldn't do anything but knock her right back down.

Gunnah grabbed his plate of heroin off of the table and tooted two lines. He sat it back down, and laughed as the drug coursed through his blood stream. "Nawl, shawty, dat shit right durr ain't gon' fly. Bitch, you lying." He grabbed a handful of her hair and pulled her up. "I called every jail in Memphis, and ain't none of dem bitches had you in 'em, so what you talkin' 'bout?" He pulled harder.

"I wasn't in Memphis. I was locked up in Harris County. I hit some bitch over the head with a bottle in my brother's club. He tried to post bail immediately, but they weren't going. They tried to charge me with attempted murder and all dat shit." She winced in pain as his hold got harder. "Please, Gunnah."

Gunnah shook his head again. "Nawl bitch, see dat durr ain't gon' fly either. You gon' have to come way better den dat." He slammed her against the wall and grabbed her neck, choking her. "Bitch, I know damn well that yo' brother would have never allowed for them white folks to have carted you away in a police car from his club. And ain't no bitch stupid enough to come at you knowing dat yo' brother is a pure savage. See, I'm tired of you thanking I'm a goofy, so I ain't got no other choice than to choke yo' ass out right here and right now. I'm through wit' you." He grabbed her neck with two hands and lifted her from the ground.

"Ack. Ack. Ack!" Skyy slapped at his hands. She couldn't breathe. Her eyes started to water. She kicked her feet wildly.

"I can't stand the thought of another nigga fucking yo' li'l pretty ass. I'd rather see you six feet under first, so dat's where you going. After I kill you, I'm coming for Jimmy next, believe dat shit." He squeezed tighter, having settled on killing her in the spur of the moment.

Skyy struggled and beat at his hands as hard as she could. She started to go weak. She stopped fighting. Her arms went slack. The room started to turn black.

"Yeah, bitch, die. Die, die, die. Don't nobody fuck wit' Gunnah. I run the world. Me, me, me. Hell yeah." He began to slob at the mouth.

Rondo slipped behind him and smacked him as hard as he could on the back of the head with the handle of his pistol. Bam! "Hell nawl, nigga, let my bitch go."

Gunnah released her and she fell to the ground gasping for air, Gunnah fell forward against the wall and table. He pushed the table aside and fell beside it. He groaned in pain. He came to his knees and touched the blood that was spurting out of his head. It ran down his neck profusely. "What the fuck?"

Rondo stood over him with eight young teens. None of them was older than fifteen, but they were loyal to him and coldhearted. Each teen had their guns drawn and were ready to kill something at Rondo's ordering. Rondo kicked, Gunnah in the ribs. "Nigga, get yo' ass up right now."

Gunnah looked up to see who had hit him. He squinted his eyes. "Rondo, you bitch-ass nigga, fuck you doing in my shit?" He groaned and tried to stand all the way up.

Rondo smacked him with the pistol again and knocked him back to the ground. "Bitch-ass nigga, what da fuck you thank you doing putting yo' hands on my shawty? You already know that's a death sentence right thurr, homeboy."

Gunnah had fallen to a pushup position. He slowly came back to his knees for a second time. He laughed with blood coming out of his mouth. “Just like you Duffle Bag Cartel bitch niggas. Always saving a hoe. Dat’s how the crew broke up to begin wit’, ain't it? Mikey mad ’cause Phoenix fucked his bitch.” He sucked his teeth and spit blood on the carpet.

“Dat shit ain't got nothing to do with me. I fuck wit’ Skyy the long way though, but it ain't just ’bout dat.” Rondo cocked his gun. “Where dat paper at, my nigga?”

Gunnah lowered his head. He knew it was coming. “So all along this bitch was setting me up? Damn.”

Skyy finally got a hold of herself. She stood up, and behind, Rondo. “You don't need him to tell you. I know where every safe he got in here is. It’s six of them, and six combinations. I just don't know which code goes to which.”

“Den we need him den.” Rondo shook his head and pressed his barrel to Gunnah's cheek. “And I ain't finna play wit’ you my nigga. Cough up dem locations for each code, or I'm smoking you right here and right now.”

“You gon' do dat shit anyway. I'd be a damn fool to give you those codes and you kill me anyway. I might as well go out like a champion and leave my funds where only my Sniper Gang niggas can get to it.”

“Oh yeah?” Rondo asked.

“Yeah, my nigga,” Gunnah returned.

“Awright, we gon' see ’bout dat.” Rondo kicked him as hard as he could in the chest and knocked the wind out of him. “Pick his punk ass up, duct tape him. We gon' see how tough he is after we torture dat ass for an hour or better. And while we're torturing dis nigga, Skyy, you gon' take dese codes and try dem out on each safe until dem bitches pop one at a time. If all of dem pop before he give dem up, dis nigga is fish food. Now get to it.”

He texted Jimmy Bands letting him know what was about to go down. He made sure that he put it in such a way that solely Jimmy would understand. As soon as the message was over, he slid on his black leather gloves and lowered his eyes, in kill mode. Now was the time to earn his stripes. This was the leader of Orange Mound. If he killed him, there was nothing on the books that said he couldn't inherit the turf. It was his homeland, all he knew, and all he cared about outside of his young crew of bloodthirsty savages that he'd formed around him for purposes such as this.

***

They sat Gunnah in a chair and duct taped him securely to it. He struggled against the bonds cursing loudly, yet incoherently because the tape was so tight over his mouth. Snot poured out of his nose. Rondo came and leaned into his face with a sneer across his mug. He grabbed him by the neck and dug his nails into his flesh until blood appeared around it.

Skyy stood next to him, breathing hard. “Damn, Rondo, I tried all of the codes on dis one safe and so far, it ain't budge. I thank dis fool might’ve switched them or something.” She was nervous and praying that she hadn't sent Rondo and his crew of animals off on a blank mission.

Rondo pulled the gloves tighter on his fingers, and looked down on Gunnah. “Dat’s all good, li'l one, ’cause dis fool finna tell us where everythang at, ain't dat right, Gunnah? Shake yo’ head if you are willing to comply?”

Gunnah kept his head still. He growled inside of the tape. He was moving so much that his chair squeaked across the basement floor, the wood of the legs threatening to splinter and break.

Skyy yanked the tape from his face. “Say, mane, don't nobody wanna kill yo goofy ass. Why don't you just give us the right combinations so we can be up out of here? You ain't doing nothing but playing with yo' life."

Gunnah spit at her. "Fuck you, bitch. I'd rather die than to put any more bread in yo' pocket. Rondo, I hope you know you dealing wit' a straight gold digger. Dis bitch don't are 'bout you, me or nobody else, not even Jimmy. All she care about is the Almighty dolla. That's on everythang." He mugged her.

Skyy punched him so hard in the nose that it broke upward. Blood began to spill into his lap. "You talk too ma'fuckin' much. Always trying to make shit out to be more den what it is. Just give up the combinations so we can be up out of here."

Gunnah pulled his head back as blood ran down his neck and all over his cheeks. He struggled to breathe. He spit on the floor. "You're a cold piece of work, Skyy. But it's cool. One day you gon' get yours, shawty. Best believe dat."

Rondo' walked up to him with a pair of vice grips in his hand. "Say, playboy, we ain't got time for all of dis. You either finna tell me what's the combinations or I'm finna go down in history as torturing and getting down on the Sniper Gang's head. What's it gon' be?"

Gunnah looked at the floor. "A coward dies a thousand deaths, and a real nigga like me can only die once."

"Fuck dat mean, nigga?" Rondo got closer.

"Take it how you want to," Gunnah spat.

Rondo nodded. "Awright, we finna see. Hold his head." Rondo waited until two of his shooters came over and took a hold of Gunnah's head. As soon as it was secure, Rondo opened the vice grips before clamping them on to Gunnah's cheek. He tightened the grips as tight as he could and began to pull.

Chapter 19

"Ahhhhhhhhhhh! Ahhhhhhhh! What the fuck is wrong with you? Ahhhhhhhhhh!" Gunnah hollered before Skyy smacked the tape back over his mouth. Blood poured out of his missing cheek like an overflowing volcano.

Rondo held his cheek out for him to see it dangling from the vice grips. "See dis shit here, mane? What you gon' do?"

Gunnah stomped his feet on the ground as hard as he could. Tears ran down his face and mixed with the blood that was already there. He shook his head and bucked his eyes wide open.

"Betta play ball den, nigga." Skyy ripped the tape from his mouth.

Gunnah struggled to catch his breath. "Look, mane, I ain't giving y'all all of my shit. I'll give up half. I can't give up all because it doesn't belong to me. It ain't my money."

"Yeah, dis nigga wanna play games. Slap dat shit back over his mouth, mane," Rondo ordered.

Skyy did just that. "I can tell he finna cave. Claw him up again," she said, acting like the scene going on in front of her wasn't freaking her out as much as it was.

Rondo clamped the vice grips on to the tip of Gunnah's nose and tightened the claws. Once they were tightened, he began to pull with all of his might. Gunnah went crazy as he felt the skin break on both sides of his nose. He heard the flesh tearing and he fainted. When Skyy slapped him awake again, Rondo was standing in front of him holding the tip of his nose with plasma leaking from it.

"Let's see what he got to say now." Skyy pulled the tape from his face, and in the midst of doing so, wound up with blood all over her wrist and knuckles.

"Okay, man, okay. Fuck dis shit, but I'm telling you right now dat you don't understand. All da money dat you 'bout to take from me doesn't belong to me. It belongs to Jimmy Bands. Dis all his shit. Once he find out what y'all done did, he gon' kill yo' ass, Rondo, and yo' punk ass too, Skyy."

Rondo was thrown off. "Jimmy Bands? Nigga, you a ma'fuckin' lie. Jimmy don't fuck wit' Sniper Gang. That nigga Duffle Bag all day and until the world blow. Bitch, you lying."

"Call him den. Call that nigga and tell him what you doing to me and you're about to find out real fast. I bet you he tells you to leave me be. If he doesn't, you can smoke me right here and right now." Gunnah said this with his face dripping large amounts of blood.

"You know what? I'm fin' too." He pulled out his cell phone, ready to dial.

Skyy saw an abundance of cash flying out the window and had to stop the fiasco before it got started. Even if Gunnah was telling the truth, they were in too deep. She didn't give a fuck if the money belonged to Jimmy Bands or not. She wanted it. She grabbed Rondo's wrist. "Wait, baby, fuck calling Jimmy. He doesn't even like discussing bidness over da phone like dat. If all of this money is his, we can just give it to him later, but for now, let's finish the mission. Ain't yo' crew starving?"

Rondo looked around at his crew of hungry, starving, damn near broke teens. Most of them were from low income housing, and the others were homeless. They needed this score, and he had to make it happen. If the money belonged to Jimmy Bands, he could always hit him with it later after asking for a percentage for his homies. "Yeah, you right. Look, Gunnah, the next thang I'ma do is rip yo' eyelids off. Give me the combination and direct me to the safes, or it's a wrap. What you gon' do?"

Gunnah closed his eyes. "I'll take you all over the house and give you what you want. Fuck Jimmy's money, dis shit ain't worth me dying over."

Skyy smiled. "Good answer."

***

It took twenty minutes for Rondo and his crew to locate and empty out every single vault inside of the safe house. By the time they were finished, they had come up on 1.5 million dollars in cash, twenty kilos of heroin, and fifteen of coke. Rondo loaded up his whips with the spoils and came back to the basement. "Looks like you were a good sport. Dat shit was in yo' best interest."

Skyy came down the steps and stood beside Rondo. "What we gon' do wit' his bitch ass now, baby?"

Rondo pulled his .45 out of the small of his back and cocked it. "It ain't what we 'bout to do, but what you 'bout to do." He looked over at her. "Dat nigga been beating on you since day one. Fucking you over just cause he paying a few of yo' bills. Dat's punk shit. Seems to me dat da best option is fo' you to take him out the game like he was just getting ready to do you. What you thank?"

Skyy became nervous. "I ain't never killed nobody before. I'm scared."

Rondo grabbed her to him and made her stand in front of him. "Bitch, wrap yo' hands around dis pole and let me guide yo' simple ass."

"Okay." Skyy did as she was told. She wrapped her hand around the gun and closed her eyes expecting a blast. When none came, she opened them.

Gunnah fought against his binds in his chair. Blood ran from his face and nose. He felt weak. He imagined what the bullet was going to feel like entering into his body, and he started to shake. He was afraid of death.

Rondo guided the gun until it was pointed right at Gunnah's face. "Awright, shawty, thank 'bout all dem times dis nigga beat you or forced himself on you. Thank 'bout all dem times you hated yo'self after he climbed from yo' body. Den thank 'bout if he would have killed you just a li'l while ago."

Skyy frowned. Her heart began to beat harder and harder. "I hate you, Gunnah! I hate yo' stinking guts."

"Yeah, baby, hate dat nigga." Rondo ripped the tape from Gunnah's mouth. "Nigga, beg for yo' life. Maybe we'll save you."

"Please don't kill me. Please. I'm sorry, Skyy. I swear I'll never beat you again. I apologize, please."

"Yuck, nigga." Rondo slapped the duct tape back over his mouth. "Awright, you heard him beg. Now it's time to finish this nigga. Let's get it." Rondo placed his hands on top of hers, took her finger, and pulled the trigger, sending a bullet into Gunnah's Adam's apple.

Gunnah's head jerked backward and snapped his neck. He was dead as soon as the impact happened. The room splashed red at first, and then faded to black.

"Shoot that nigga again, baby," Rondo urged. He removed his finger this time

Skyy pulled the trigger again and again and again with her eyes closed. When she opened them, Gunnah was slumped over with his brains hanging out of his face like spaghetti. She sighed and jumped back.

Rondo mugged Gunnah's corpse. "Rest in blood, nigga."

That night, Jimmy Bands was still out of town on business. Rondo took it upon himself to send his loyal killas all around Orange Mound, door to door, knocking off loose members of the Sniper Gang. Before the night was concluded, thirty-one

Sniper Gang members had been killed, and over fifty had fled the hood with their lives intact for the moment.

***

When Jimmy Bands found out about the death of Gunnah, and how he had been stripped, he went ballistic. He grabbed May Baby and Rondo and rushed over to where Gunnah's body was. It had been kept in the same position, and everything. It had been found by two of Jimmy Bands' security team that rolled through to collect the funds that Gunnah had accrued for the week. When they got there, they'd found Gunnah stretched out and the house ransacked. Instead of contacting the local authorities, they hit up Jimmy and waited until he flew in from Port Au Prince, Haiti before they made another move.

Rondo played the situation close to his chest. He wanted to see what was really going on before he made his next move. He strolled about the house as if he had never been there before, shadowing Jimmy Bands.

Jimmy Bands squatted down in front of Gunnah's body and shook his head. "Fuck! Ain't dis 'bout a bitch?"

Rondo shook his head as he stood behind Jimmy Bands. "I don't understand, Blood. Why the fuck we care if dis nigga got slumped or not? He was just talking dat dumb shit a few weeks back."

Jimmy sighed. "Yeah, but I went over his head and got shit situated. All of dis money was mine. We had conquered the Sniper Game by a simple phone call. The Mound belonged to me, and it wasn't nothing dat Phoenix could do 'bout it. Fuck. The niggas took my whole stash. Dat nigga Phoenix finna come at my head. What am I gon' do?"

May Baby came over and rubbed his shoulders. "We'll figure it out, baby. We always do. I wouldn't even worry 'bout it."

Jimmy Bands lowered his head again. "I gotta find out who did this shit, and I gotta whack they ass after I get my shit back. Ain't no way I can rebound from dis shit right hurr, mane. Only way I can is if I get my shit back. Fuck!" He punched his hand as hard as he could.

"Yeah, mane, well, you already know I'm wit' you. Just let me know what you wanna do, and we gon' get to it. Ride or die my nigga." Rondo pulled his nose and sniffed hard.

Jimmy Bands nodded and stood up. He faced Rondo and placed his hands on his shoulders. "Say mane, you help me find out who did dis and I got ten G's for you, li'l dawg. Hit the streets and bring me back that definite, and it's yours. What you say?"

"Ten G's? All of dat for me?" Rondo laughed. "Yeah, awright, nigga, dat sound like a bet." Rondo removed Jimmy Bands' hands off of his shoulders. "Before I go though, I need to know one thang."

"Damn, nigga, time is money. Fuck you wanna know?" Jimmy Bands muttered, irritated.

Rondo laughed a killer's laugh. "Dat nigga Phoenix was yo' big homie, right?

"Yeah, of course he was," Jimmy assured him.

"And he was feeding you and yo' family, and all of dat shit, right?" Rondo asked.

"Yeah, dat's a good nigga." Jimmy Bands had to admit.

"And you mean to tell me dat you lost all of his money, and all of yours too?" Rondo stepped back a tad.

"What, man? Hell nawl. I still got five million of my own money put up. I ain't dat stupid. Dat nigga shit just fucked off.

That's crazy though." Jimmy thought about his next move, and knew it had to be his best one.

"Yeah, it is crazy, 'cause I gotta have all of dat, my nigga."

Rondo upped two F&Ns and placed them to Jimmy Bands' face. His young armed goons came from all over the house and filled the living room, laying May Baby on her back with their guns aimed at her and Jimmy Bands.

"Nigga, I want all of dat bread, and everythang you got left. When I'm done wit' you, I'm stripping Phoenix too and smoking you niggas. There is a new day in Orange Mound, and there is a new leader of this here Cartel, and his mutha-fuckin' name is Rondo."

Chapter 20

"And once again our top story today is that there are thirty-four confirmed cases of Coronavirus at the White House, including the President of the United States. Sources close to the White House say that the President's staff has been deeply affected by the virus, and many are very sick. Those that have come back with positive tests but are showing no symptoms are made to quarantine for the recommended fourteen days. When asked if those that are affected will be able to carry out their duties, the White House Correspondent declined to comment. In other news—"

Natalia took the remote from Taurus's hand and cut off the television. She stood in front of the screen with a smile on her face. "Well, Daddy, are you proud of me?" She knelt down in front of him while he sat on the couch.

"What did you do, baby?" He looked down at her and placed his right hand on the side of her beautiful face.

"I did the opposite of what they wanted you to do. They wanted you to infect our people: the disenfranchised, the poor, and the defenseless. Well, I flipped the script and gave them a taste of their own medicine, and it didn't even cost me that much." She laughed. "You would be surprised at how much pull your baby girl really has when it comes to Russia and the Kremlin." She placed her hands on his knees. "So are you proud of me, Daddy?"

Taurus stood up. He stepped past her and looked out of the window. "Baby, you just opened up a can of worms." He started to shake. His mind was racing so fast that he couldn't even think straight. He thought about all of the powers in Washington. He thought about all of those shiesty, racist, egotistical, angry, vindictive people, and he knew that Natalia had no idea what he was up against.

Natalia came behind him and hugged his body. "Daddy, I know that the only reason they freed you from prison and faked your death is because they wanted you to work for them by infecting and killing off our people. I know that because they saved your life that you are indebted to them. You are not the first man that has had a connection to Russia and have gotten off from committing a serious crime. But there is also something else that you don't know." She turned him around so that he could look into her bright blue eyes.

Taurus held her face, he was still shaking. "What else, baby? What else don't I know?"

"You don't know my mother is the one that pulled the strings for you to be released. You don't know that from the moment you stepped foot out of those prison walls, I knew you were out, and every second since then I've been trying to find you for myself. I didn't kill my mother until I knew that you were free."

Taurus frowned. "So you really did kill Nastia?"

Natalia nodded. "She raised me to believe that you were a sick and perverted man. She made me feel that the Black side of me was tainted, and because of it, that I would never be anything more than evil. She told me that I was the devil's spawn, and because of her, I grew up with a complex." She started to cry. "She hated me because I was mixed. Up there in Russia, they hated me as well. They called me names and raped me, even with my mother's knowledge. They did this under the guise of it being the Russian way. My mother actually wanted them to fuck the Black out of me, and I hated her for it. But the more they tried, and the worse things got. All it did was make me yearn for you - my father. When I found information that told me that she was looking to get you out of prison so that you could commit genocide on your own people, and so that she could secretly be with you behind the

Kremlin's back, I snapped. I don’t regret it because all I've ever wanted was you.” Natalia kissed his lips and shook her head. “He's no longer in debt to Putin. It cost me more than four hundred million, and don't ask me where I got it from, but it’s paid. You are no longer in debt to the White House, and he is no longer in debt to Putin. We are free, and once again all I want is you.” She hugged him.

Taurus hugged her back and rested his chin on top of her head. “Damn, baby, you did all of that for yo’ daddy?” He was at a loss for words.

She nodded. “Yes. I exhausted a lot of resources, and I am low now, but I don't care. All I want is you, and you are all that matters to me, outside of Junior.”

Jahliyah pushed open the door and placed her hand on her hip. “Well, here y'all go again. What type of party are y'all having around this piece?”

Natalia backed off of Taurus and shot daggers at Jahliyah. “Don't you know how to knock?”

Jahliyah ignored her. “Daddy, this is what you're doing now? You're fuckin' with your own daughter on some sick shit? Really?”

Natalia hurried and stood within Jahliyah's face. “Listen to me, Jahliyah, you don't have the slightest clue of what you're dealing with, but if I was you, I would back up and leave while your life is still intact.”

Jahliyah took her earrings out of her ears. “Look, I know I come off all demure and shit, but what but what you fail to realize is that I was born and raised in Orange Mound. I had my first fight when I was eight years old, and I ain't lost one yet. Bitch, you're about to find out real fast that I am my mother's daughter.” She placed her earrings in her pocket and pushed Natalia as hard as she could out of her face. “Get the fuck out of my face.”

Natalia flew backward over the bed and wound up on her back. She bonked her head on the floor and holler out in pain. "Bitch!"

Taurus jumped in the middle of them. "What the fuck is wrong with you two? Y'all are sisters!"

Jahliyah pointed at Natalia as she got up off of the floor. "Tell her that. She's the one that keeps coming at me all disrespectful and shit. I don't care what y'all got going on. That doesn't got shit to do wit' me. You're my father too, and I love you." She hugged him.

Once again, Phoenix stood at a safe distance while he watched the scene unfold. At its duration, he had plans to move on Taurus. First he would lure him into a vulnerable space, and then he and his Duffle Bag Cartel would torture him until he gave up all of his wealth. Once that goal was achieved, Phoenix had visions of making Taurus pay the ultimate penalty. His legacy would be no more, and finally, Phoenix would reign as the sole king of the Stevens family and its bloodline.

Natalia was both embarrassed and infuriated. She saw Jahliyah wrap her arms around Taurus and she snapped. She slipped her hand under the mattress of the bed and grabbed her .9 millimeter.

"You trying to take my daddy away from me, bitch? Well, that ain't happening. Over my dead body."

She jumped up with the gun in her hand and anger flowing through her veins. She aimed the gun at Jahliyah and squeezed.

***

Rondo and twenty cars pulled up to the back of Phoenix's mansion and jumped out of their cars, heavily armed. Rondo kept the shotgun pressed into the back of Jimmy Bands' head as he guided him to the back door of the mansion. He had already stripped him of his millions and now Phoenix was next. Rondo was hungry for the crown and was ready to meet death in order to obtain it. “Keep walking, bitch nigga. We almost there.”

Jimmy Bands kept his hands in the air. “I'm doing everything you tell me to. All I ask is that you don't kill me.”

Skyy kicked Jimmy in his ass. “Shut up, bro. I ain't never known yo’ ass too be this soft.”

“Bitch, I'm yo’ brother, and dis how you do me? Where is your loyalty?” Jimmy asked, hurt.

Rondo laughed. “A bitch gon' always be loyal to the money. Never forget that.” He tossed Jimmy Bands through the back door of the mansion just as two shots went off upstairs.

“What the fuck?” Skyy hollered, falling to the ground.

To Be Continued...
Duflle Bag Cartel 6
Coming Soon

Submission Guideline

Submit the first three chapters of your completed manuscript to ldpsubmissions@gmail.com, subject line: Your book's title. The manuscript must be in a .doc file and sent as an attachment. Document should be in Times New Roman, double spaced and in size 12 font. Also, provide your synopsis and full contact information. If sending multiple submissions, they must each be in a separate email.

Have a story but no way to send it electronically? You can still submit to LDP/Ca$h Presents. Send in the first three chapters, written or typed, of your completed manuscript to:

LDP: Submissions Dept
Po Box 944
Stockbridge, Ga 30281

DO NOT send original manuscript. Must be a duplicate.

Provide your synopsis and a cover letter containing your full contact information.

Thanks for considering LDP and Ca$h Presents.

Coming Soon from Lock Down Publications/Ca$h Presents

BOW DOWN TO MY GANGSTA

By **Ca$h**

TORN BETWEEN TWO

By **Coffee**

THE STREETS STAINED MY SOUL **II**

By **Marcellus Allen**

BLOOD OF A BOSS **VI**

SHADOWS OF THE GAME II

By **Askari**

LOYAL TO THE GAME **IV**

By **T.J. & Jelissa**

IF LOVING YOU IS WRONG… **III**

By **Jelissa**

TRUE SAVAGE **VII**

MIDNIGHT CARTEL III

DOPE BOY MAGIC IV

CITY OF KINGZ II

By **Chris Green**

BLAST FOR ME **III**

A SAVAGE DOPEBOY III

CUTTHROAT MAFIA III

DUFFLE BAG CARTEL VI

By **Ghost**

A HUSTLER'S DECEIT III

KILL ZONE **II**

BAE BELONGS TO ME III

A DOPE BOY'S QUEEN III

By **Aryanna**

COKE KINGS V

KING OF THE TRAP II

By **T.J. Edwards**

GORILLAZ IN THE BAY V

3X KRAZY II

De'Kari

THE STREETS ARE CALLING II

Duquie Wilson

KINGPIN KILLAZ IV

STREET KINGS III

PAID IN BLOOD III

CARTEL KILLAZ IV

DOPE GODS III

Hood Rich

SINS OF A HUSTLA II

ASAD

KINGZ OF THE GAME VI

Playa Ray

SLAUGHTER GANG IV

RUTHLESS HEART IV

By Willie Slaughter

THE HEART OF A SAVAGE III

By Jibril Williams

FUK SHYT II

By Blakk Diamond

THE REALEST KILLAZ III

By Tranay Adams

TRAP GOD III

By Troublesome

YAYO IV

GHOST MOB

Stilloan Robinson

KINGPIN DREAMS III

By Paper Boi Rari

CREAM II

By Yolanda Moore

SON OF A DOPE FIEND III

By Renta

FOREVER GANGSTA II

GLOCKS ON SATIN SHEETS III

By Adrian Dulan

LOYALTY AIN'T PROMISED III

By Keith Williams

THE PRICE YOU PAY FOR LOVE II

By Destiny Skai

CONFESSIONS OF A GANGSTA III

By Nicholas Lock

I'M NOTHING WITHOUT HIS LOVE II

SINS OF A THUG II

By Monet Dragun

LIFE OF A SAVAGE IV

MURDA SEASON IV

GANGLAND CARTEL III

By **Romell Tukes**

QUIET MONEY III

THUG LIFE II

By **Trai'Quan**

THE STREETS MADE ME III

By **Larry D. Wright**

THE ULTIMATE SACRIFICE VI

IF YOU CROSS ME ONCE II

ANGEL III

By **Anthony Fields**

FRIEND OR FOE III

By **Mimi**

SAVAGE STORMS II

By **Meesha**

BLOOD ON THE MONEY II

By J-Blunt

THE STREETS WILL NEVER CLOSE II

By K'ajji

NIGHTMARES OF A HUSTLA II

By King Dream

THE WIFEY I USED TO BE II

By Nicole Goosby

IN THE ARM OF HIS BOSS

By Jamila

Available Now

RESTRAINING ORDER **I & II**

By **CA$H & Coffee**

LOVE KNOWS NO BOUNDARIES **I II & III**

By **Coffee**

RAISED AS A GOON I, II, III & IV

BRED BY THE SLUMS I, II, III

BLAST FOR ME I & II

ROTTEN TO THE CORE I II III

A BRONX TALE I, II, III

DUFFLE BAG CARTEL I II III IV V

HEARTLESS GOON I II III IV

A SAVAGE DOPEBOY I II

HEARTLESS GOON I II III

DRUG LORDS I II III

CUTTHROAT MAFIA I II

By **Ghost**

LAY IT DOWN **I & II**

LAST OF A DYING BREED

BLOOD STAINS OF A SHOTTA I & II III

By **Jamaica**

LOYAL TO THE GAME I II III

LIFE OF SIN I, II III

By **TJ & Jelissa**

BLOODY COMMAS I & II

SKI MASK CARTEL I II & III

KING OF NEW YORK I II,III IV V

RISE TO POWER I II III

COKE KINGS I II III IV

BORN HEARTLESS I II III IV

KING OF THE TRAP

By **T.J. Edwards**

IF LOVING HIM IS WRONG…I & II

LOVE ME EVEN WHEN IT HURTS I II III

By **Jelissa**

WHEN THE STREETS CLAP BACK I & II III

THE HEART OF A SAVAGE I II

By **Jibril Williams**

A DISTINGUISHED THUG STOLE MY HEART I II & III

LOVE SHOULDN'T HURT I II III IV

RENEGADE BOYS I II III IV

PAID IN KARMA I II III

SAVAGE STORMS

By **Meesha**

A GANGSTER'S CODE I &, II III

A GANGSTER'S SYN I II III

THE SAVAGE LIFE I II III

CHAINED TO THE STREETS I II III

BLOOD ON THE MONEY

By J-Blunt

PUSH IT TO THE LIMIT

By **Bre' Hayes**

BLOOD OF A BOSS **I, II, III, IV, V**

SHADOWS OF THE GAME

By **Askari**

THE STREETS BLEED MURDER **I, II & III**

THE HEART OF A GANGSTA I II& III

By **Jerry Jackson**

CUM FOR ME I II III IV V VI

An **LDP Erotica Collaboration**

BRIDE OF A HUSTLA **I II & II**

THE FETTI GIRLS **I, II& III**

CORRUPTED BY A GANGSTA I, II III, IV

BLINDED BY HIS LOVE

THE PRICE YOU PAY FOR LOVE

DOPE GIRL MAGIC I II III

By **Destiny Skai**

WHEN A GOOD GIRL GOES BAD

By **Adrienne**

THE COST OF LOYALTY I II III

By Kweli

A GANGSTER'S REVENGE **I II III & IV**

THE BOSS MAN'S DAUGHTERS I II III IV V

A SAVAGE LOVE **I & II**

BAE BELONGS TO ME I II

A HUSTLER'S DECEIT I, II, III

WHAT BAD BITCHES DO I, II, III

SOUL OF A MONSTER I II III

KILL ZONE

A DOPE BOY'S QUEEN I II

By **Aryanna**

A KINGPIN'S AMBITON

A KINGPIN'S AMBITION **II**

I MURDER FOR THE DOUGH

By **Ambitious**

TRUE SAVAGE I II III IV V VI

DOPE BOY MAGIC I, II, III

MIDNIGHT CARTEL I II

CITY OF KINGZ

By **Chris Green**

A DOPEBOY'S PRAYER

By **Eddie "Wolf" Lee**

THE KING CARTEL **I, II & III**

By **Frank Gresham**

THESE NIGGAS AIN'T LOYAL **I, II & III**

By **Nikki Tee**

GANGSTA SHYT **I II &III**

By **CATO**

THE ULTIMATE BETRAYAL

By **Phoenix**

BOSS'N UP **I , II & III**

By **Royal Nicole**

I LOVE YOU TO DEATH

By Destiny J

I RIDE FOR MY HITTA

I STILL RIDE FOR MY HITTA

By **Misty Holt**

LOVE & CHASIN' PAPER

By **Qay Crockett**

TO DIE IN VAIN

SINS OF A HUSTLA

By **ASAD**

BROOKLYN HUSTLAZ

By **Boogsy Morina**

BROOKLYN ON LOCK I & II

By **Sonovia**

GANGSTA CITY

By **Teddy Duke**

A DRUG KING AND HIS DIAMOND I & II III

A DOPEMAN'S RICHES

HER MAN, MINE'S TOO I, II

CASH MONEY HO'S

THE WIFEY I USED TO BE

By Nicole Goosby

TRAPHOUSE KING **I II & III**

KINGPIN KILLAZ I II III

STREET KINGS I II

PAID IN BLOOD **I II**

CARTEL KILLAZ I II III

DOPE GODS I II

By **Hood Rich**

LIPSTICK KILLAH **I, II, III**

CRIME OF PASSION I II & III

FRIEND OR FOE I II

By **Mimi**

STEADY MOBBN' **I, II, III**

THE STREETS STAINED MY SOUL

By **Marcellus Allen**

WHO SHOT YA **I, II, III**

SON OF A DOPE FIEND I II

Renta

GORILLAZ IN THE BAY **I II III IV**

TEARS OF A GANGSTA I II

3X KRAZY

DE'KARI

TRIGGADALE I II III

Elijah R. Freeman

GOD BLESS THE TRAPPERS I, II, III

THESE SCANDALOUS STREETS I, II, III

FEAR MY GANGSTA I, II, III IV, V

THESE STREETS DON'T LOVE NOBODY I, II

BURY ME A G I, II, III, IV, V

A GANGSTA'S EMPIRE I, II, III, IV

THE DOPEMAN'S BODYGAURD I II

THE REALEST KILLAZ I II

Tranay Adams

THE STREETS ARE CALLING

Duquie Wilson

MARRIED TO A BOSS… I II III

By Destiny Skai & Chris Green

KINGZ OF THE GAME I II III IV V

Playa Ray

SLAUGHTER GANG I II III

RUTHLESS HEART I II III

By Willie Slaughter

FUK SHYT

By Blakk Diamond

DON'T F#CK WITH MY HEART I II

By Linnea

ADDICTED TO THE DRAMA I II III

IN THE ARM OF HIS BOSS II

By Jamila

YAYO I II III

A SHOOTER'S AMBITION I II

By S. Allen

TRAP GOD I II

By Troublesome

FOREVER GANGSTA

GLOCKS ON SATIN SHEETS I II

By Adrian Dulan

TOE TAGZ I II III

By Ah'Million

KINGPIN DREAMS I II

By Paper Boi Rari

CONFESSIONS OF A GANGSTA I II

By Nicholas Lock

I'M NOTHING WITHOUT HIS LOVE

SINS OF A THUG

By Monet Dragun

CAUGHT UP IN THE LIFE I II III

By Robert Baptiste

NEW TO THE GAME I II III

By **Malik D. Rice**

LIFE OF A SAVAGE I II III

A GANGSTA'S QUR'AN I II III

MURDA SEASON I II III

GANGLAND CARTEL I II

By **Romell Tukes**

LOYALTY AIN'T PROMISED I II

By Keith Williams

QUIET MONEY I II

THUG LIFE

By **Trai'Quan**

THE STREETS MADE ME I II

By **Larry D. Wright**

THE ULTIMATE SACRIFICE I, II, III, IV, V

KHADIFI

IF YOU CROSS ME ONCE

ANGEL I II

By **Anthony Fields**

THE LIFE OF A HOOD STAR

By Ca$h & Rashia Wilson

THE STREETS WILL NEVER CLOSE

By K'ajji

CREAM

By Yolanda Moore

NIGHTMARES OF A HUSTLA

By King Dream

BOOKS BY LDP'S CEO, CA$H

TRUST IN NO MAN

TRUST IN NO MAN 2

TRUST IN NO MAN 3

BONDED BY BLOOD

SHORTY GOT A THUG

THUGS CRY

THUGS CRY 2

THUGS CRY 3

TRUST NO BITCH

TRUST NO BITCH 2

TRUST NO BITCH 3

TIL MY CASKET DROPS

RESTRAINING ORDER

RESTRAINING ORDER 2

IN LOVE WITH A CONVICT

LIFE OF A HOOD STAR

Printed in the USA
CPSIA information can be obtained
at www.ICGtesting.com
LVHW020407120424
777133LV00037B/894

9 781952 936661